Teach's Light

A Chapel Hill Book

Teach's Light

A Tale of Blackbeard the Pirate

by Nell Wise Wechter

Illustrated by Bruce Tucker

The University of North Carolina Press

Chapel Hill and London

First published by
The University of North Carolina Press in 1999
Copyright © 1974 by Marcia Wechter Kass
Originally published in 1974 by John F. Blair
Manufactured in the United States of America

The paper in this book meets the guidelines for
permanence and durability of the Committee on
Production Guidelines for Book Longevity
of the Council on Library Resources.

Library of Congress Cataloging-in-Publication Data
Wechter, Nell Wise. Teach's light:
A tale of Blackbeard the pirate / by Nell Wise Wechter;
illustrated by Bruce Tucker. p. cm.
SUMMARY: Determined to find the source of the fabled light
that supposedly guards Blackbeard's treasure, two Outer
Banks teenagers suddenly find themselves transported back
to 1681 into the life and times of the notorious pirate.
ISBN 0-8078-4793-3 (pbk.: alk. paper)
1. Teach, Edward, d. 1718—Juvenile fiction.
[1. Blackbeard, d. 1718—Fiction.   2. Pirates—Fiction.
3. Time travel—Fiction.   4. Ocracoke Island (N.C.)—
Fiction.]   I. Tucker, Bruce, ill.   II. Title.
PZ7.W4125 Te   1999   [Fic]—ddc21   99-13505   CIP

03 02 01 00 99   5 4 3 2 1

For my grandsons

Casey Bob

and

Travis Lane

Two little pirates
who'll be bent and bound
to go looking for
Teach's Light

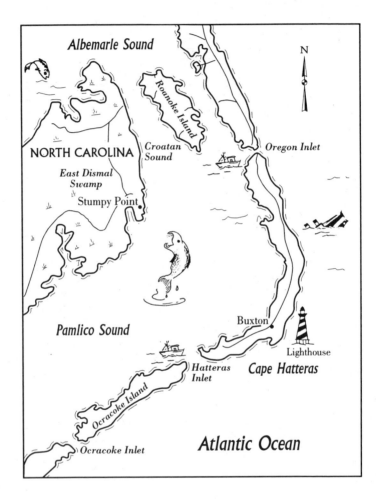

Albemarle Sound

N

Roanoke Island

NORTH CAROLINA

Croatan
Sound

Oregon Inlet

East Dismal
Swamp

Stumpy Point

Buxton

Lighthouse

Pamlico Sound

Hatteras
Inlet

Cape Hatteras

Ocracoke Island

Ocracoke Inlet

Atlantic Ocean

INTRODUCTION

THE LEGEND of Teach's Light has been handed down by the natives of Stumpy Point village in Dare County, North Carolina, for three centuries.

Across the Bay—an arm of Pamlico Sound—lies Little Dismal Swamp. It is over this swamp that the light appears. According to legend, the light guards one of the many treasures buried by Edward Teach, alias Blackbeard, the infamous pirate.

The light is always seen in the same general location. Sometimes it hovers; sometimes it "bobbles." It is not seen with any regularity. Nobody can foretell when it will appear. When the atmosphere is especially clear, the light looms in glorious splendor.

Youngsters and oldsters alike see it. When it does appear, they watch it and wonder: "Will Teach's Light just hover, or will it do a Devil Dance?"

Time present and time past
Are both perhaps present in time future,
And time future contained in time past.

—T. S. ELIOT

Four Quartets

CHAPTER ONE

The day before yesterday always has been a glamor day. The present is prosaic. Time colors history as it does a meerschaum pipe. —VINCENT STARRETT

"TEACH'S LIGHT is really cutting didoes tonight," Fran Davis said as he laid down his pipe on the coffee table. Toby, his son, and Corky Calhoun, the next-door neighbor girl, sat on the screened-in porch with Mr. Davis. The three of them had been talking since suppertime about the things they planned to do during the coming summer—camping expeditions, beach outings, and prospective trips to New England and Canada.

Toby slipped his hassock closer to the window. "Man alive," he squealed, "look at that light. It's bobbling up and down like a satellite out of orbit."

"Atmospheric conditions are probably just right this evening for the light to be visible," Mr. Davis replied. "Strange thing, Teach's Light." He shook his head, silently wondering what caused the phenomenon.

"It looks like a round stingray with dancing legs," Corky said, laughing.

"Golly, just think of all the years the light has been seen across the Bay over Little Dismal Swamp," Toby marveled.

"People around these parts have been seeing it for nearly three hundred years," Mr. Davis told them. "Through the centuries, folks have handed down the yarn that the bobbing light is guarding one of Blackbeard's treasures, which the pirate supposedly buried somewhere on the fringes of Little Dismal."

"Yeah, I know," Toby answered. "It's curious why the light always seems to stay in the same general place. Maybe it *is* guarding some of Blackbeard's booty. Or, perhaps it's trying to show folks where the treasure really is buried."

"For mercy sakes, Toby." Corky laughed derisively. "You don't still hold with that old tale Grandpop used to tell us when we were little, do you?"

"Well, now, your grandfather surely seemed to believe there was something peculiar about Teach's Light," Toby affirmed.

"Grandpop was a seafaring man, and old salts like him sometimes had a superstitious streak in them. I can just see Grandpop in my mind's eye, taking out his brass telescope—long glass he called it—adjusting it to our eyes, and telling us to look closely and we might even see Teach's ghost dancing in front of the light. If I remember correctly, your behavior and mine around Grandpop was pretty good for several hours thereafter," Corky said, chuckling.

"You can't prove that your grandfather didn't know what he was talking about, now can you?" Toby insisted. "Teach's Light is still in the same place it was then, isn't it? Hey, I know what. Why don't you go home and get that spyglass so we can look at the light?" Excitement caught Toby up, making his eyes sparkle.

"All right," Corky told him, catching his enthusiasm. "It won't take a minute. The glass is hanging on the wall by my bed. That's where I put it when Grandpop passed away. Its being there on the wall sort of makes me feel that a little part of Grandpop is still around." She sighed, and then was out of the Davis porch and had gone across the yard to her own house.

Toby jumped up and went inside the house to his bedroom, where he pulled a map off his desk and got an old-time compass and protractor set out of a drawer. By that time Corky was back.

"Let me have it, please," Toby requested, taking the big brass instrument. "Golly," he said, squinting at the dim letters on the telescope. "This thing was made by Dixie Limited, London, in 1600."

"It's old," Corky agreed. "Grandpop said that it was a nautical glass which probably came off one of the early English privateers."

"I'll bet it did, too," Mr. Davis told them, taking a look at the lettering.

"Could have," Corky said. "Grandpop made lots of voyages to England and down in the Caribbean. He was always bringing home odd things. Our barn has one corner full of ships' lanterns, binnacles, quadrants, and all kinds of seafaring stuff."

Toby pulled the glass out to full length. The lens was excellent. In a second or two he had the telescope adjusted to his sight. "Man, oh, man," he said, breathing in an awed way, "look at that light go!" He handed the glass to Corky for a look, while he plastered his face to the screen and stared at the dancing light across the Bay.

"Young people," Mr. Davis told them, "I'm going to leave you with your legends of Blackbeard and his dancing light and go join Mrs. Davis at the television set. It won't be too long now before the summer reruns start and TV will be a bore for another three months. Now, Toby," he said, winking at Corky and grinning, "you get that treasure map all fixed up so when Dr. Calhoun and I get ready to take you kids deer-hunting with us this fall, you can take your map and lead us right straight to Blackbeard's loot!" He roared with laughter as he closed the screen door behind him.

"Your dad is a real tease," Corky said. Like Mr. Davis, she held no strong beliefs about the light over the swamp. She accepted the fact that it was there and did not really pay it very much mind.

"Dad doesn't hold with any of the old legends," Toby told her. "Black is black, and white is white. There isn't any gray where he is concerned. I wish he would believe in some of the stories," he said, sighing plaintively.

"He's a realist instead of a romantic like you," Corky told him. She took another squint through the glass. "It surely makes a person wonder though—that crazy light—

bobbing over the swamp all these years without anybody coming up with any answers of how or why it's there. Yep, it surely does make a body wonder."

"I know that legends are folk tales that many people label pure fiction," Toby said, frowning. "But how about the legend of how Nags Head got its name? That's not so farfetched. And that Lost Lady—Theodosia Burr—off Kill Devil? And what about the story of Virginia Dare and the Lost Colony? Seems to me that people in the olden days had so much work to do just to keep alive that they didn't have time to make up a pack of lies to tell about such things. I believe in Teach's Light. There's got to be something true about it, or it just wouldn't stay there in the same place for three hundred years. What do you think?"

"I don't know what I really think," Corky told him, wrinkling her brow in deep thought. "I believe in ESP and intuition, and sometimes I know I have premonitions that come true. Lots of people would call that believing in the supernatural and would certainly call me some kind of a nut. I surely do agree that there's something eerie about Teach's Light. What it is, I can't even begin to guess. But Toby, it does seem a little far out to believe that an inanimate thing like a light is guarding a treasure. I can't seem to swallow that bit."

Toby frowned. It was plain he did not entirely agree with her thinking. "Some pirate ships were wrecked before their crews could save the booty crammed in the holds," he told her. "Just the other day I read about some divers finding a lot of treasure in an old Spanish wreck off the Florida Keys."

"Granted," Corky said, nodding her agreement. "But the newspaper certainly didn't say a word about any crazy light hovering over the water to guide the divers to the treasure," she told him, grinning.

"Okeh," Toby said forlornly, feeling that he was losing his argument. However, he was determined to bring in all the points he could. "How about what Dr. Hugh Rankin wrote in his book about pirates in colonial Carolina? He said that sometimes when a band of pirates were brought to bay and were preparing to fight their way out, they would hide their loot ashore on the eve of battle if they didn't want to be caught with the goods. Dr. Rankin also wrote that many pirates had such successful cruises they actually had to put some of their plunder ashore and bury it. Now, how come Blackbeard couldn't have done just that?" Toby demanded earnestly.

"You certainly have a good point," Corky returned. Interest shone in her face. "Like Captain Flood," she said, remembering. "He was a pirate who held out on his crew and hid extra amounts above his share. Then, later, he went back to the hiding places and got his booty. But even if Blackbeard did hide some of his treasures, that's still no explanation for the light over the swamp."

"Toby! Corky!" Mrs. Davis called from the house. "Looks like a good movie coming up now on television."

But Toby and Corky were oblivious to everything except their own animated conversation and Teach's Light, which was putting on a first-class show of its own against the wide screen of the dark sky over Little Dismal.

There was another who watched Teach's Light!

As he watched, a great wave of agitation shook his tall body. The man was old and grizzled; still he seemed of great strength. His blue eyes shot madness that was cold as a Norwegian fjord. His thin-lipped mouth was cruel-looking, and it sat like a gash between his strong jaws. At the moment, he stood among scattered crab pots at the unkempt landing where he kept his shove-skiff. Back a few yards was his shack, which he had built of driftwood and debris which constantly washed up on the sandy shore of Casey's Point on the edge of Little Dismal Swamp.

The man raised his arms and shook his fists at Teach's Light. Sometimes the light was a ball and seemed to hover over the shack, casting weird, moving shadows over the rough structure. Then, long tentacles of brilliance seemed to run down to the trees, where they twined with the branches.

"By the beard of St. Olaf!" He roared out the Norwegian oath to the heavens. "It's the damned *Allemands** setting Heaven afire with their flying machines. The box! I must get the secret box."

*Germans

He turned and walked rapidly to the shack, where he blew out a kerosene lantern that sat on an orange crate. Then he hurried out and closed the door of the shack behind him.

Nels Sven, dubbed the "Mad Russian" by the natives on the village side of the Bay, was really a Norwegian. He dated back to World War II. Very little, in fact, was known about him, but the villagers believed that he was crazier than a bedbug in kerosene. They were glad that Sven lived on the opposite side of the Bay from the village. Even so, his very presence, anywhere near the village, was an unpleasantness to them.

Old though Sven might be, he now pursued his way on a path that was hidden by a thicket of gall bushes. He moved like a shadow, a falling leaf, a stalking panther.

Down at the base of a giant cypress, he squatted and, with dextrous hands, began digging. The soft, peaty soil made next to no sound as it flew out and hit the earth.

"Ach, the box!" he said exultantly, the madness in his eyes intensifying as he pulled the box out by its handle.

He pressed to his breast the packet he had dug up. The color, in the moonlight, seemed a dull gray. Teach's Light danced over him, sending shimmering prongs of light down upon him.

"German devils," he cursed, shaking his fist at the light. "Sven will give you a taste of Loki's thunder. Your iron hunters will feel the steel of Sven's box."

Then, like a wraith, Sven disappeared through the

edge of Little Dismal. Like a teasing will-o'-the-wisp,
Teach's Light, above the trees, seemed to bobble over
the "Mad Russian."

CHAPTER TWO

May you go safe tonight
With stars and space above, and
Time and stars below.
—LORD DUNSANY

Up, lad; when the journey's over
There'll be Time enough to sleep.
—A. E. HOUSMAN

"I'LL GET the card table so we can have a place for all this stuff," Toby said. He handed the telescope to Corky and began to lift out the table from the corner of the porch.

"You're quite gung-ho about Teach's Light, aren't you, old friend?" Corky asked, laughter flashing from her black eyes. "Did you hear how your dad poked fun at us when he went into the house just now?" A good-natured grin spread across her rosy cheeks. "I reckon that laugh of his told us what he really thinks about Teach's Light guarding any treasure." She sighed, remembering some of the old tales her grandfather had told her about his seafaring life and about the legends of the Walter Raleigh Coastland, particularly about Teach's Light, since it was right in their midst. She missed her grandfather, who had died some years previously. Again she sighed, bringing her attention back to Toby and the card table he was unfolding.

"Be back in a minute," Toby said. "Got to find some colored pencils and get them sharpened so we can use them on the map." He darted through the living-room door to look for the items.

Corky arranged her tall, well-proportioned body more comfortably in the straight chair, which she slid up close to the card table. She straightened out the map which Toby had brought from his room, spreading it across the table.

Even though she was seventeen, two years older than Toby, and two grades ahead of him in school, Corky never in any way acted superior or conceited to her friend. In fact, she did not feel conscious of their difference in age. She also seemed oblivious of the twelfth-grade fellows at her school who labeled her a "slick chick." She participated in several of the honors classes at Manteo High School and was active in extracurricular activities. She was an excellent swimmer and a good athlete, preferring the joys of baseball and basketball, or deer-hunting, or crab-potting with Toby to spending all her leisure time in just dating the fellows. However, she was not antisocial. Far from it. She liked to dance, and she never lacked for partners when the crowd on many days stopped off at the Teeners' Joint after school.

Corky was an only child of retired parents. Dr. Calhoun, her father, after his navy retirement, had been appointed by the President to the Water and Air Resources Board, a position that required much traveling up and down the eastern seaboard. It was as if he had not retired at all, Corky sometimes felt. Her mother was a retired registered nurse, who worked at the Dare County Medical Center in Manteo. Corky had learned early to be self-sufficient and independent. Her grandfather had been a great source of joy to her. He had been her maternal grandfather, and many times Corky's mother had declared that "Papa is going to make a boy out of Corky yet!" When her grandfather died, Corky was dreadfully sad. She still missed the genial old man who had helped to make her growing up pleasant.

The Calhouns were next-door neighbors of the Francis Davises. Mr. Davis owned a large shrimp fleet, which plied Pamlico Sound, the waters off Ocracoke, and in the fall of the year when the big green-tailed shrimp came, the Atlantic Ocean off Brunswick, Georgia. Pam Davis, his wife and Toby's mother, was a lovely South Carolina belle, who was wont to spoil Toby and Corky by doing many nice things for them. There certainly seemed to be no generation gap between the parents and young people of the Davis and Calhoun families.

When Toby turned fourteen, Fran Davis had given his son a fiberglass boat with an outboard motor. There was not an inlet or a cove within a twenty-mile radius of the village that Toby and Corky had not explored both day and night. When the youngsters tuned up for crab pots of their own, their parents had bought them some. Toby and Corky fished the pots after school and made their own spending money.

Toby was a ninth-grader, and he excelled in history. It was his favorite subject, next to physical education. His tall, wiry body made him a natural on the basketball court. Happiness shone out of his clear blue eyes and, most of the time, his face carried an easy grin, which exposed a mouthful of white teeth. The ninth-grade girls vied for his favor, but Toby seemed oblivious. He thought of Corky as the "nice-girl-fellow" who lived next door—his best friend and staunchest ally, even though they argued so loud and hard at times that the grownups yelled at them to "cool it." Through the seventh and eighth grades, Toby's English grammar and new math had certainly been made smoother because of Corky's jogging him over the rough places. In his turn, Toby had many times had in his files history help for Corky when she needed a particular piece of research.

The old legends of North Carolina and its Outer Banks were Toby's real joy. For the past three years his history project had been to collect as many legends and old stories as he could find and to tape-record all the ones that the old people of the village told him. His bookshelves held several scrapbooks and tape racks. Naturally, the legend of Teach's Light held prominence, because all Toby had to do, many nights, was to go on the front porch of his own house and there it was—Teach's Light —bobbing over the trees in Little Dismal across the Bay.

"Well, sir," Toby puffed, as he came out to the porch, "the darned pencil sharpener fell apart, and I had to sharpen all these pencils with the butcher knife. That's what took me so long."

"The thought came to me that you'd had a conniption fit and had fallen into it," Corky said. "This is some job you've done on the map," she told him admiringly. "Really looks like a genuine treasure map. Very professional, sir!"

"It's part of the history project," Toby told her. "It's as accurate as I know how to make it. I've marked all the places where Edward Teach might have landed. The Bay here is part of Pamlico Sound, and Blackbeard darted in and out of coves all over Pamlico Sound, up this way as well as farther south. So, let Dad make fun of the map and legends. I believe what the old folks say about Teach's Light," he affirmed. "Nobody's come up with any answers about it, and nobody's found any pirate loot over there where the light is. I tell you, Corky, Teach's Light has some reason for being there. Boy, look at it now. It's doing a regular chicken strut!"

"It surely is," Corky agreed, taking a look and then stifling back a yawn. "Lots of folks look on Teach's Light like they do the legend of the Phantom Hoofprints at Bath or the tale of the Devil's Tramping Ground in

Chatham County. One of these days, they say, scientists will come up with the reasons for all the unexplained lights floating around and the dents which the devil and ghost-horses supposedly make in the earth. Perhaps a space satellite will take pictures of the unexplained things and will telephoto them back to earth."

"Yeah," Toby said. "That really is possible. But do you remember what your grandpop told us about St. Elmo's Fire, and how the early seafarers were so frightened of it?"

"Certainly I do," Corky answered, her black eyes sparkling. "Seafarers made Elmo the patron saint of sailors. So? What's that got to do with Teach's Light?"

"So! Miss Corky Calhoun, isn't St. Elmo's Fire still a phenomenon? Has anybody ever really solved the riddle of why that happens?"

"Partially, I think," Corky said, wrinkling her forehead in thought. "It seems to me that, from my physics, I remember something about corona discharge at the surface of a conductor—something about ionization of the surrounding atmosphere."

Toby seemed crestfallen at losing a point. He had not yet had physics or chemistry in school. Corky was good at both subjects. He knew she wouldn't fool him.

"There's something romantic about St. Elmo's Fire," she went on. "But I get the jimjams looking at that crazy light over there bobbing up and down, particularly when

I think about the horrible creature that Blackbeard was. Thoughts of that bloodthirsty pirate would give a saint the creeps."

"Well, I think the secret of Teach's Light is solvable, too," Toby said, "and I think it's got something to do with treasure. Hey, Corky," he suddenly blurted. He hesitated, gulped, and began again: "Say, Corky, I dare you to let's take my boat right now and strike out across the Bay, take this telescope with us, and see if we can't locate the exact place where Teach's Light hangs over the Swamp. Nighttime has to be the time to find the location. Can't be done in daylight. Look through the glass right now. See? The light is quite close to the edge of the Bay. What do you say, Cork? Come on. Let's go! Right this minute!"

"Toby Davis, have you lost your ever-loving mind!" Corky exclaimed.

"No, ma'am, Miss Corcoran Catherine Calhoun, I have not," Toby affirmed.

Corky nervously adjusted the telescope to her eyes. "Well, for goodness sakes," she said, "it's nearly nine o'clock. And you know Casey's Point is no place for us to be traipsing around in at night without any grown-ups." Her hands fidgeted with the telescope, and her heart beat with a flutter at Toby's proposition. But she was determined to talk both their ways out. "What in the world would your folks say? And mine, if they were home? You know Mother and Dad are in Wilmington tonight and Mrs. Canutti is staying at the house with me. That good lady would have a litter of polecats if she thought we even had such a notion." Tingles of electrical excitement raced up and down her nerve endings. She and Toby had talked many times about going on such an expedition, but this was the closest they'd ever come.

"Shucks, my folks wouldn't think anything if they heard my outboard start up right now. We've gone boating in the moonlight with them and your folks and by ourselves a dozen times in the past. We'll yell and tell them we're going to take a spin around the Bay. I know they won't say a word against it. It's a pretty moonlit night, and there isn't a speck of wind to bother. Come on," he cajoled. "Darn it, I know you aren't any sissy. We'll never have a better chance than we've got right now to really locate the place of Teach's Light. I double DARE you! And anybody that'll take a dare will . . ."

"Eat a rotten mare," Corky finished the old rhyme for him. A quake of dread ran through her. "What if we run into the 'Mad Russian'?" In the back of her mind, Corky knew it was dread of Nels Sven that held her back. She respected the dangers of rattlesnakes and water moccasins; she stood in awe of waterspouts and the hurricanes that hit the coast. But if there was one thing on earth she stood in mortal fear of, it was Nels Sven. The madness in his eyes petrified her. She could never rationalize her aversion. "Nels Sven rambles all over Casey's Point day and night," she went on. "You know what a close shave we had with him last fall—that afternoon he thought we were setting our crab pots too near his. I tell you, Toby, I don't want to be within a country mile of that old gent. A person just can't tell what he will do. Ugh," she said, shivering in distaste and dread.

"Well," Toby offered, "when we get nearly across the Bay, we'll look and see if the lamp is burning in Sven's shack. If it is, then we'll know he's up. We'll cut off the outboard and row very quietly the rest of the way. When we get close to the landing, we'll pussyfoot—not make a sound. If his light is out, then we'll know he's gone to bed," Toby argued reasonably.

"That's just maybe-so—his being abed," Corky told him worriedly. "I wonder if Sven ever sleeps. He walks around like a zombie, except for that horrible madness in his eyes. I'll bet he's got bear traps set all around that landing, too. How'd you like to step into one of those contraptions in the dark?"

"Aw, you're just borrowing trouble," Toby argued. "We can watch carefully where we walk. Both of us know how hunters fix bear traps, and we'll be able to see and stay away from them. I tell you, Corky, this is the time to go and try to unravel the mystery of Teach's Light. And if we did, boy, oh, boy, would we ever be famous!"

Corky snorted in derision. Still, her heart pounded and her nerve endings prickled with excitement.

Toby noticed that she was edging off the sofa to get

out from behind the card table. He watched her in expectancy.

When she got out from behind the table, she stood up to full height, put her arms akimbo, and with black eyes flashing fire, she addressed her friend:

"We'll go," she said, letting her breath out in a shudder. "But it's the craziest thing I've ever let you talk me into. Four years ago, against my better judgment, I let you talk me into helping you build a tree house in the brittle branches of your weeping willow tree. Both of us knew better, and we certainly found out better, for sure, when the branches started snapping off, sending house and about six of us crashing to the ground. Boy, some of your ideas are real lulus, and I reckon I'm the world's biggest nut to fall in with them. Man, oh, man," she gulped, emotion nearly closing her throat, "if we get back in a whole piece from this jaunt, I aim to have my Daddy-doctor examine both our heads. Provided the men in white coats haven't already come and taken us away!"

"WHOO-pee!" Toby started to yell, thought better of it, and tried swallowing his misbehaving Adam's apple. Happiness shone from his eyes. "Cork's a REAL guy," he thought to himself. He rubbed his clammy hands against his jeans, and his blue eyes batted in excitement. "Dad and Mother are so buried in television," he said, peeping through the porch window, "that a sonic boom wouldn't faze them. But I'll holler and tell them."

"We're going to take a spin in the outboard," he yelled through the window. Mr. Davis did hear. He nodded his head that it was all right.

"Darn it, Toby Davis, I hope you realize the fool thing we're setting out to do," Corky said, holding her tummy. It felt as if cold, clammy eels were running relays up and down her insides. In the back of her subconscious there was also the feeling of the cold madness that glared from the eyes of Nels Sven.

At the moment, Toby was too excited for any dread. "You bet I know what we're doing," he sputtered in joy. "We're going to find the place of Teach's Light."

CHAPTER THREE

*Time goes by turns, and chances change by course.
From foul to fair, from better, hap to worse.*
                                          —ROBERT SOUTHWELL

THEY MADE their way out to the ditch that lay between the Calhoun and Davis lots and joined the canal
that ran back of the village. Toby's boat was moored to
the footbridge.

"This zany outing has to be the craziest, most lunatic
notion that any so-called intelligent boy and girl have
ever dreamed up," Corky fussed, as she helped Toby
guide the fiberglass boat down the wide ditch. "I can
just hear my mother quoting William Butler Yeats:
'Youth is a silly, vapid state,' etc. . . . etc. . . . And this is a
time I'd agree with her wholeheartedly. Really, Toby,
it is getting late. Tomorrow is a school morning, too.
What you say we finesse it? We'll go hunting Teach's
Light another time."

"Aw, Corky, you said you'd go, and we're already on
the way," Toby wheedled. "We've been talking about
doing this very thing for a long time. It's a pretty, warm,
moonlit night. Like I said, we won't ever have a better
chance than this. You really scared? I have never heard
you argue so like a dingbat."

"Watch your language, Toby Davis!" she said, bristling. "You know darned well I'm scared. And so are you! I'm only trying to point out some common sense to both of us. Sure, I'd like to know the secret of Teach's Light. But just suppose we do run into Nels Sven? That's what's really worrying me. It's the danger from the *living* rather than from the supernatural that's bugging me. You know Sven is loco—always mumbling in his broken English about folks trying to find his secret box and steal it."

"What do you reckon he's got in that silly old box he's always yakking about?" Toby asked, as he pulled the rope on the outboard. The motor caught, and the trim little craft went skimming down the wide canal that entered the Bay.

"Who in the world gives a hoot?" Corky retorted. "That man is nuttier than a fruitcake. He ought to be put away. He's dangerous—a menace—I think." She shivered.

"He's a doozy all right," Toby agreed. "I know there are all kinds of tales told about him in our village. I wonder if anybody really knows a speck of truth about him."

"I believe Grandpop did," Corky answered.

"Like what?" Toby inquired.

"Grandpop was a seafarer. Old salts like him usually knew a whole lot about the sea and ships, as well as stories about other seamen."

"True," Toby said, nodding his agreement. "What did he say about Sven?"

"After Grandpop retired from the sea, he often visited an old buddy of his, who had also retired from the maritime service and had settled on Cape Hatteras. Sometime, during the month of February, 1942, Grandpop went over to Cape Hatteras to visit his friend. The old-timers had duck-hunted at Buxton every winter since their retirement. But World War II was in full swing and ship sinkings off Cape Hatteras that year were running high, so the government had banned all hunting on the island. Grandpop went for his annual visit anyway. It turned out to be quite an exciting week. Two or three convoys were torpedoed off Rodanthe, and the night before Grandpop was to come home, a Norwegian tanker was sunk about ten miles offshore, right opposite the beach house where Grandpop's friend lived."

"Wow!" Toby exclaimed. He had read about the ship sinkings off Cape Hatteras. Corky's tale had brought them close enough to make his skin crawl.

"Well," Corky went on, "Grandpop said the Cape Point coastguardsmen rescued four or five survivors from the Norwegian ship. They found Sven clinging to a piece of wreckage. And guess what?"

"Well, what?" Toby asked.

"Strapped to Sven's body was a gray, waterproof box."

"Son of a gun!"

"He wouldn't let anybody touch the box. Even when he was carried to the coast guard station, he wouldn't let the box out of his sight."

"Didn't anybody ask him about the box? Why didn't somebody open it?"

"He couldn't speak a word of English. Anyway, I suppose the coastguardsmen figured that Norway was a friendly nation and that whatever Sven had in his box was none of their business. For want of a name, the coastguardsmen dubbed Sven the 'Mad Russian.' He was like a wild man, they said, particularly if anybody went close to his box."

"Did your grandfather see Sven while he was on his visit?"

"Oh, no," Corky answered. "Civilians weren't allowed on the coast guard compound. I think that Grandpop's friend told him later on about Sven."

"Told him what?"

"Well, after a day or two, Sven just vanished from the Cape Point coast guard station."

"Vanished? Where in the world to?" Toby wrinkled his forehead in perplexity. "In those days, Cape Hatteras didn't have a highway; there wasn't a bridge across Oregon Inlet—just an old wooden-tub ferryboat. How in the dickens did he get off Cape Hatteras without anybody knowing?"

"Oh, he's cunning as a fox, as you very well know. It's a mystery how and when he left Cape Hatteras. He must have moved like a shadow and kept himself away from human habitation for a long time."

"Yes, he's sly," Toby agreed. "It's a mystery to me how he landed at Casey's Point and when he came there."

"Well, you were about four and I was about six, I think, when those hunters at Casey's Point accidentally stumbled on Sven and his shack. I believe that was the first time the folks in the village knew anything about Sven's being over there."

"Folks say those hunters very nearly got a dose of buckshot that Sven turned loose at them from that double-barreled shotgun of his. The 'Mad Russian' probably thought they were after his secret box."

"I imagine so," Corky agreed.

"I remember one morning Mother sent me down to Mr. Jack's store. Sven was there. He had shoved his skiff across and had come to buy something. Anyway, Mr. Leland was at the store, too, and he was trying to talk to Sven. Sven was waving his arms around and squalling something in a mixture of Norwegian and German about the *Allemand*s, *donner*, *jagers*, *stahl*, and a *packet*. I don't imagine I'm saying those words right, but Mr. Leland knows a smattering of Norwegian and German. He said the 'Mad Russian' was cussing the Germans and swearing he was going to send thunder out of his steel box on the German iron hunters in the sky. Boy, you ought to have seen Sven's eyes. They were blazing with hatred and madness. He grabbed whatever he had bought and stamped out in a fury, cursing the *Allemand*s in his crazy lingo. Mr. Leland looked at Mr. Jack and remarked that he was glad that old Norwegian didn't come over to the village very often, and Mr. Jack said that he was darned happy that he wasn't a German if Sven was going to be around. I know Sven scared me half to death that morning."

"He hates Germans—that's for sure," Corky agreed. "I guess he feels he has good reason since they blew him up aboard that Norwegian freighter. Then, too, the Germans invaded Norway in World War II. Do you remember reading about the incident of the *Tirpitz*?"

"I sure do," Toby answered. "Maybe the Nazis killed some of Sven's family—or all of them except him—and that's another reason he hates them so much. The bad part *now* is that he seems to think everybody is a German and is after him and his secret box. Why, he must be close to seventy years old. He's sure been hating a long time."

"He really doesn't look that old," Corky said. "I guess it's because he's so tall and so big. But he looks sneaky and furtive. I'd trust a diamondback rattlesnake quicker than I would Sven. That crazy Norwegian scares me plum silly."

"I'm not in love with him either," Toby said, frowning. "I haven't forgotten the nasty cussing he laid on us that afternoon when we rammed my boat into one of his crab pots which had sunk below the waterline."

"It's a thousand wonders he didn't shoot us right then

and there," Corky told him, her teeth chattering at the thought.

"He didn't have his shotgun in the skiff," Toby explained. "I looked. Gosh, that was a nip-and-tuck time, wasn't it? With the crab pot a-tearing a hole in my boat and us out in the middle of the Bay with the water pouring in, and you a-bailing for dear life to keep us from sinking, and that crazy Norwegian cussing and threatening us with that long, heavy oar. I thought I'd never get the wire pot pulled out of the fiberglass so I could get the outboard started. Whew! I get goose feathers just thinking about the mess we were in."

"Goosebumps, you idiot!" Corky said, with a giggling shudder. "That's the very kind of danger I've been trying to get through your thick noggin—about our going over to Casey's Point now—tonight. It was daylight when all that crab-pot mess happened. At least we could see what we were about. But like two zanies, here we go, late at night, looking for a will-o'-the-wisp pirate light when we know that after we land we'll have to walk right by Sven's place. 'O what fools these mortals be!' In my book, Sven, Edward Teach, and the Devil could all be blood brothers, and I'd just as lief stay away from them all!" A thoughtful frown wrinkled her forehead. An idea popped into her head. "Hey, give me the tiller, Toby, and let me steer awhile." She reached over eagerly to grasp the steering post.

"Ha, not on your life," Toby said, with a wide grin.

"Why, you'd turn this boat around and head for home so fast it would make our heads swim. We're over halfway across now. Look at Teach's Light bobbing over there. I tell you and tell you right over and over we won't ever have such an opportunity again."

"Yes," Corky answered, drawing a long, shuddering sigh. "But there's a coiling thing in my tummy trying to unwind, and I'm perspiring ice water. Call me chicken, if you want to, but I'm plum scared out of my wits, Toby. Not of Teach's Light, of course, but of Sven."

"Well, if it's any satisfaction for you to know, I've got a few screamie-meemies pawing at me too. But there's something stronger than fear in my brain a-pushing around."

"That's loose nuts and bolts rolling around in your bean," Corky told him. She reached into the waterproof boatbox where Toby kept life rings, flashlights, and tools and pulled out the brass telescope. She focused it against the bobbing light. "Boy," she squealed, "Teach's Light looks close enough to touch. It's hovering over the trees right at the edge of the Bay there."

"That's what I told you before we left the house," Toby reminded, as new excitement caught at him. He cut down the speed of the outboard to a near purr. "Seems to be hovering over that long spit on the east side," he said, squinting through the moonlight. "I don't see any reason in the world why we can't pinpoint its exact location. We might even find some pirate loot," he said seriously. "Stranger things have happened."

"Toby Davis," Corky wailed, "you CANNOT possibly believe that Teach's Light is guarding any treasure. That is just too far out for anybody's credence."

"How come I can't believe it?" Toby countered solemnly. "I know you are older and smarter than I am, but you listen and check me if I am wrong: Didn't we learn in North Carolina history that no treasure was found on Blackbeard's sloop after he was killed? That no gold or silver or jewels were found in any of the pirate storehouses at Bath or Ocracoke?"

"Correct. So?" Corky wondered what he was getting at.

"Well, what happened to all that pirate booty? I think Teach and his crew buried a lot of it, in several different places. One of the places could be right here on the shoreline of Little Dismal. One of the legends I collected says that an old Ocracoke sea dog thought he knew the answer about some of Blackbeard's loot."

"How's that?" Corky's curiosity was gradually replacing some of her fear.

"The old salt was helping the pirate careen his ship one day, and he got bold enough to ask Blackbeard if he had ever told any of his wives where he buried his treasures. Blackbeard said: 'Nobody but me and the Devil knows where me booty's hid. And the longest liver, be it me er the Devil, shall take it all. The brimstone of Hell will hover over me booty, and villains better beware.' That hovering, bobbing light over there may not be brimstone, but darned if I don't think it's some kind of a sign," Toby insisted. His chin set stubbornly.

"Man, oh, man, how superstitious can you get?" Corky asked, shaking her head in bafflement at Toby's firmness. You *know* that most of the plunder taken by pirates off the North American coast and the Caribbean was taken to colonial ports and sold. The colonial merchants found that pirate goods provided a good way of getting around the hated English custom duties and trade laws."

"Yep. We studied that last year in Mr. Rogers' history class," Toby agreed. "And I also know the quartermasters divided the proceeds of the booty among the pirate crew. Many of them spent all they received carousing and merrymaking in the nearest tavern. But that doesn't mean that all the pirates did that. Some of them could have buried some treasure."

"I have a feeling that the tales of buried treasure have become a very exaggerated notion about pirates—like that old tale of pirates making their captives walk the plank. It's storybook stuff, Toby. Just think about Edward Teach for a minute. Wasn't he a notorious spendthrift and wastrel? I doubt if he had enough of anything accumulated to bury anywhere. Oh, he liked to brag and make folks believe big things about himself; and he was

so mean and cruel that the coastal folks were scared half
to death not to take for law and gospel everything the
braggart said."

"I'll go along with you on most of what you said just
then," Toby told her. "But how about those small sea
chests of jewels and pieces of eight and doubloons Teach
was always snatching from the rich Spanish ships down
in the Caribbean? If I remember my history, Blackbeard

gave one of those chests to Governor Eden after one of his cutthroat voyages."

"Okeh," Corky said, conceding the point, "but all that still doesn't explain Teach's Light. Speaking of lights, look. Sven's light is out." She breathed a little easier.

"I noticed," Toby answered. "But I'm going to cut off the motor just the same. We'll paddle the rest of the way." He picked up a paddle and passed it to Corky, taking another for himself. "We'd better talk in low tones. Voices carry quite loudly over water on a still night like this. I'll bet old Sven is snoring in Norwegian right about now," he said, grinning.

"I hope he's as solid asleep as Rip Van Winkle slept those twenty years," Corky said, shivering again. "Nobody can ever be sure about that old codger. He might be out chasing Teach's Light tonight, swearing the Germans are after him and his box. I bet a nickel Teach's Light sends him into a fury." She stared through the night at Sven's darkened shack.

Moonlight shimmered like diamonds on the Bay. Stillness hung over them like a blanket except for the "ribbets-fry-bacon-tea-tables" coming from the throats of thousands of spring frogs. Toby and Corky cut the water with silent strokes of their paddles. Teach's Light seemed to bob in cadence to the music of the frogs.

"As I was saying," Toby went on in a low voice, "I believe small sea chests were buried by some of the pirates. Teach could have buried some too. Pirates' futures were very uncertain. Why wouldn't they hide some booty—like you said about Captain Flood—against the day they retired from pirating. Why couldn't they bury little caches of Spanish gold and jewels—stuff like that that wasn't too bunglesome and was worth a lot of money? Sounds reasonable to me."

"Did you ever hear of any pirate dying a rich man?" Corky asked with a disdainful snort.

"Yes, ma'am," Toby said vehemently. "What about Benjamin Hornigold?"

Corky grimaced, knowing Toby had bested her. "Well, he accepted the King's pardon and stopped being a pirate. So he doesn't count," she said, grinning lamely.

Toby chuckled with glee. "Got you that time, didn't I? Well, Blackbeard got his pirating start under Hornigold. I'll bet he showed Blackbeard a hundred places to hide loot and just as many tricky ways to hide it, too. That crazy light over there might even be a trick of some kind."

"Toby! Toby! You are just too much!" she told him. "You're an incurable romantic whom no amount of common sense will ever ever cure. If romanticism were contagious, I think I'd like to catch some. Maybe then I wouldn't be covered with these goosebumps. The closer we get to shore, the more I pepper out with cold bumps."

"They're Sven bumps," Toby said teasingly. He was

sorry he had said it the moment it left his mouth. The back of his own neck began to prickle.

A mullet jumped near the outboard with a great splash. Both Toby and Corky were so startled they nearly lost their paddles. But they said nothing and cut the water swiftly.

"Well," Toby finally gulped, "I reckon Sven's secret box and Blackbeard's loot can't be too far apart over here. If we don't find one, maybe we'll find the other."

Corky paddled furiously in fearful exasperation. Toby was hopeless!

The boat slipped quietly into the cove of the spit of sand. Moonlight and Teach's Light made the landing outstandingly plain.

"I'll moor the boat to this cypress," Toby said, quietly fastening the painter securely to the gnarled tree. "Get the big flashlight, Cork. I'm going to take the .22 rifle. We might run into a bobcat." He made sure he had extra bullets in his shirt pocket. He then checked the rifle to make sure the safety was on.

Corky buttoned up her windbreaker and rolled up her faded jeans to her boot tops. Toby did the same. Both of them had vinyl gloves. Briars and scraggly branches could be a menace to hands. Their deer-hunting expeditions in the past had taught them a great deal about body protection and woodcraft. Toby reached down and pulled a small flashlight out of the boat box. He shoved it into his back pocket along with a box of waterproof matches.

"Oh, brother," he said softly, "look at Teach's Light over those trees. It looks like a flying saucer with prongs on it. Maybe it's even got little green men," he said, giggling.

"It looks as if it's moved back farther over the swamp," Corky told him, watching the light jounce up and down like a crazed June bug. "Well," she offered, "if it's got little green men, I hope they stay put." Her laugh was a nervous titter.

"It's not moved back very much," Toby said, careening his neck to look. "Come on this way. Looks like an old deer path here. Let's follow it and see where it takes us. Looks as if it heads in the direction the light is traveling."

Like a will-o'-the-wisp, Teach's Light lured them. One minute it seemed to settle in the top of a tree or over one. Next, it bobbed like a cork, running back and forth over the pines and junipers like typewriter lines over a page.

So intent were they on their forward progress that they did not look behind them. So enrapt were they in their strange mission of the bobbing light that they paid no attention to the flickering shadows in the moonlight around them.

It was not strange, therefore, that they did not notice a tall, furtive shadow that dodged in and out from behind the trees.

The rough path began to widen into some sort of clearing.

Behind, the wraithlike thing kept a steady pace, then seemed to veer suddenly toward the opposite side of the clearing. It assumed grotesque shapes in the moonlit surroundings, as if something were added to its upper outline—something solid-looking, a compactness of some kind.

An owl hooted in the vastness of Little Dismal. Corky and Toby swallowed the kinky fear in their throats and walked slowly into the small clearing, at the end of which stood a giant tree over which Teach's Light had come to rest.

The shadow disappeared behind a tombstone, which stood white and stark on the opposite side of the clearing.

CHAPTER FOUR

I saw Eternity the other night
Like a great ring of pure and endless light,
All calm as it was bright;
And round beneath, Time, in hours, days, years,
Driven by the spheres,
Like a vast shadow moved, in which the world
And all her train were hurled.

—HENRY VAUGHAN

THE PATH in the clearing began to slope downward. The trees became taller and thicker. Toby and Corky moved quietly through the moonlight. The young people carefully tested their footing with each step. The earth was spongy, uncertain, and wet. Ahead of them they could see black water spread around the roots of cypress trees in low hummocks matted with vegetation.

The moonlight through the trees began to dim. There was a fetid smell of wetness and decay. Gray beards of Spanish moss festooned gnarled trees and caught at Toby's and Corky's hair as they passed under the tree branches. Poison ivy curled around jaggedly-broken branches that touched the ground. Junipers, pines, and water oaks encircled the open space. The acrid tang of wet leaves and the resinous odor of the pines bit into Toby's lungs. He gulped back a coughing spasm which puffed his cheeks out and made his breath short. Corky nodded silent approval to his valiant effort, understanding fully Toby's allergy to woods odors.

Both young people felt an uncomfortable strangeness in the atmosphere around them. A lone, bleached-white tombstone opposite them added its eerie contribution to the setting. Each wondered who in the world could have been buried way out here on the edge of Little Dismal.

"Maybe one of Blackbeard's wives," Toby thought to himself, as pin prickles stuck him in the back.

Corky shivered as Teach's Light suddenly darted over the trees and made the tombstone loom up like the Wright Memorial.

Toby pushed his mop of blond Buster Brown hair away from his sweaty face. Corky shoved up tighter the rubber band that held back her own thick mane of brown hair.

They stopped in the clearing and looked at each other. Their faces were solemn. Their eyes were round with dread, anticipation, doubt, and foreboding. Their hearts beat like triphammers. Yet, their determination was undiminished. The light, they saw, had now come over a tall juniper just ahead of them. It bobbed lazily. They looked at it in wonder. It seemed so close, as if it were reaching out and pulling at them with wanton mockery. They nodded soberly to each other. After all their times of talking and planning and plotting on the map and using the big brass telescope, could this be it? Was this the place of Teach's Light?

A nebulous shadow slipped out from behind the tombstone, gliding silently but surely until it was abreast of Toby and Corky on the opposite side. The shadow lengthened, it shortened, it hovered—like a dire malediction, like the shade of a lost soul looking for peace. Suddenly, it wavered. One long scarecrow arm stretched out before it; the other arm appeared to clasp something to its breast. The indefinite shape seemed to trip. Then, like a wraith, it began to float earthward.

A sudden blast like that of a concussion grenade encompassed Toby and Corky and sent them hurtling through space. It was as if they had been caught up in a monstrous, infernal Thing of unbelievable speed and light—a Thing that spewed out exhausts of suffocating, burning sulphur and gas which permeated the atmosphere. Blinding streaks of brilliance like that from a launching pad shot over the clearing, briefly touching, on the ground, an indistinctness of broken lines—lines that once might have formed a shadow but that now seemed to disintegrate quickly.

Above the clearing, the scintillating brilliance of the Thing—the Light sphere—sucked in Toby and Corky like a giant centripetal force and glued them to the whirling phenomenon. They became objects within an object which smashed through the temporal barrier and began to make Time chronology, as Toby and Corky knew it, meaningless.

The orbit of the Light-force was marked with a bril-

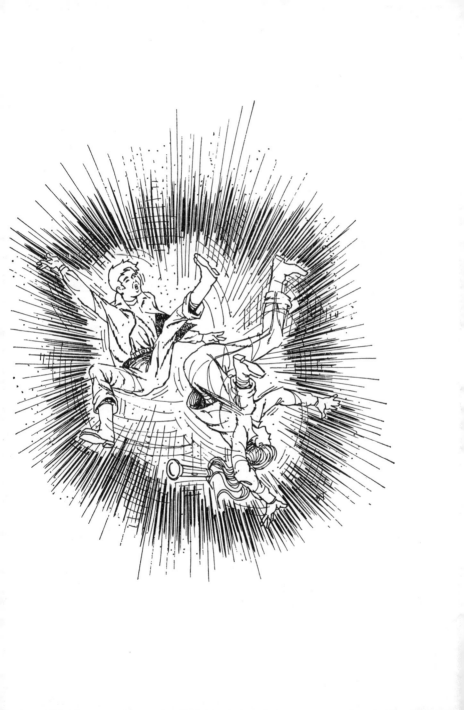

liance of so startling an intensity and of such speed that Toby's and Corky's thought patterns seemed cast through a scrambler—a scrambler made of chips of pure crystal which began to cause an exchange of telepathic emissions between them. Caught within the confines of a brilliance which was featureless and without limit, which exploded into silent colors, the two young people had sensations of being swept swiftly, irresistibly forward while impressions flashed past. They saw fields, streams, towns, cities of tall buildings, standing armies, great navies, and gardens and parks of multicolored flowers. Their thought processes made wrenching efforts to adjust to the relentless, building pressure that their breach through Time was causing. Ripples like internal tickles coursed through them as their bodies adjusted and moved parallel to the lines of temporal force instead of cutting across them.

Knowledge flowed through Corky's thoughts; Toby's synapses, at first sluggish, awkward, and blurred, now flashed a brilliant mental communication:

"Holy Jehoshaphat!" his telepathy spluttered. "How many centuries per minute does this Light travel?"

Corky caught his message instantly. "I am afraid that I can't ESP an answer to that," her telepathy transmitted. "So I reckon we'll just have to sit back and enjoy it!"

For an unmeasurable fraction of a microsecond, Toby's thought forces churned. Then his telepathy spluttered again:

"Where to? How far? Where to? How far?"

They sped backward through pale purple, featureless space that stretched out and seemed to curve in every direction. The brilliance of the Light outstripped that of the moon. The shadows fell sharp and black in the space where the moonlight stopped with razor-edged sharpness. The Light raced backward as toward a Time beacon supplied with a homing device that reached out through both Space and Time.

Down below, the Atlantic Ocean was a vast, azure mirror tilted toward infinity.

CHAPTER FIVE

We learn that we are spirits, and that something is going on in Time.

—WINSTON CHURCHILL

GILPIN GAGE, owner and bartender of the Seawitch Pub on the Bristol waterfront, plodded and staggered his way to a high bench in front of the bar, where he sprawled out for a minute's rest. He had been up all night trying to see to it that the roistering seamen did not tear his tavern to shreds. Then, too, he had done his share, and more, of imbibing ale and rum with the merrymakers. It was no wonder that, in a moment, Gilpin fell asleep and began emitting snores that shook the rafters. But his sleep was rudely interrupted when he tried to ease his position on the high bench. He plopped to the floor, the breath all but knocked out of him. A great whirring in his ears, louder than a dozen beehives, threatened to addle his pate, and the streaks of blazing light coming through the open door of the pub blinded him.

The blazing streaks passed through the pub like a bolt of white lightning and came to rest over a grove of oaks in front of the tavern. The brilliance dimmed. However, the same gigantic Force which had held Toby and Corky and had hurled them backwards in time to the Bristol waterfront of 1681—that Force now held them in a state

44

of nearly suspended animation. They both felt their telepathic capacity, their new powers of thought transference. There was some sort of awareness in their brains of the extraordinary thing that had happened. They were able to communicate with each other by exchanging thoughts, but they were aware that the maximum effective range of their telepathy was only within the confines of the Light and its tremendous force.

"Teach's Light!" they transmitted to each other. "We have been caught up by Teach's Light!"

Whatever the reason, they had sailed free above the earth, disappearing in a new dimension and reappearing in a different century.

"Maybe Teach's Light is the Fourth Dimension," Corky's telepathy emitted. "Sometime in physics, or maybe it was science fiction, I read something about a Time Gate, or a Time Shuttle, or a Time Lock. What was it?" Her thought-force churned.

Toby sensed the questions Corky was trying to answer.

"Numero Uno. Time Shuttle," Toby instantly transmitted. "We both read the same science fiction story about time travel."

"Well," Corky telepathed, "if our contact had lasted another tenth of a millisecond, we'd be ready for the insane asylum."

Toby's telepathy was working fine, but as usual, he could not always follow Corky. What in the dickens was a millisecond? He had not yet had his school physics. Also, his vocabulary about Space and Time was somewhat limited. "It's a nuisance being so telepathic if I still have to reach," he angrily transmitted. "What the heck is a millisecond?"

"Don't worry about it," Corky transmitted. "This situation is just a state—like the absence of gravity—where there is no up or down. But for heaven's sake, look at that man down there in the tavern. He looks as if he really feels *upside down*."

Gilpin Gage felt worse than that. " 'Ells-bells," he swore. "Old Sol is trying to sizzle me." His fat cheeks larded with sweat. He shook his massive head, trying to clear his vision. He felt the Seawitch undulating like an Egyptian belly dancer. The vibrations made his flesh quiver and his gorge rise. "Be gaw," he swore again, "it's the Jedgment Day, and the Devil is pulling down the four corners of 'Ell around me ears!" Gilpin was a little drunk. He was bewildered by the buzzing noises in his head, and he was still half-blinded by the brilliant light that had starkly flashed over him. All of it together made him angry and mean. He lurched his way to the back of the bar, where he poured himself a stiff drink of grog. "Hair of the dog," he croaked, gulping down the raw spirits. Just as he awkwardly set his tankard on the bar, his bleary eyes espied a ragged urchin in the pub, inching his way toward a wall table that held fish and chips. That sight further infuriated him and sent Gilpin in a lurching, half-staggering trot toward the boy.

"Be gaw, Edward Drummond, ye flea-ridden son of Lucifer, why ain't the likes of ye toting sand to the glass-makers? Git out, ye guttersnipe. Ye're jest another beggar on the Bristol streets and a thieving wretch in me tavern. Be off with ye!" He spat a mouthful of slobber at the young child and sent his foot into the boy's backside, sending him howling down the cobblestones. The effort nearly cost Gilpin his own equilibrium.

"My name is Ned Teach," the urchin screeched back angrily, as he tripped and fell into a mess of sewage pouring into the street from the overflowing cellars of the houses which sat even with the thoroughfare.

"And how would ye know yer own name? Yer old lady switches her handle from Drummond to Thatche to Teach and back to Drummond every time she goes to work in a different scullery. Puts on mighty airs she do, fer somebody who cuts up dead geese. Whatever yer name be, ye starving, thieving wretch, git away from me tavern before I cut yer tongue out, grease back yer ears, and swallow ye."

The salty bartender swore a great oath at the boy and then swilled more rum, which ran down both his chin and his gullet. "Be gone, I say," Gilpin thundered, "I ain't aiming to feed nine-year-old beggars any more than I am old beggars." He shook his fist at the child who, on

47

picking himself up out of the squalor of the street, thumbed his nose at Gilpin and, screaming an obscenity at him, took off running as fast as he could in the direction of the Bristol waterfront.

As the grizzled bartender said, Edward Teach, nicknamed Ned by the other street mud larks, was an orphan with no known father. He was also a starving ragamuffin who lived by his wits in the late seventeenth century in Bristol, England.

And Bristol, in the seventeenth century, offered wretchedness in the extreme to the street child. Even the normally poor lived in filth and disease, with hundreds of the population dying of typhoid, exposure, starvation, rats, and the plague.

So, Ned Teach, son of a scullery maid, turned loose on the streets by the time he could walk, had learned early to provide for himself by employing ingenuity and cunning as he struggled for existence against the competition of beggars, pickpockets, and the murderous men and women who frequented the Bristol waterfront.

By the time he had reached the docks, Ned's angry, nimble mind was made up.

"I'll wait till dark," he said angrily, "and I'll stow away on the first ship that sails out of Bristol." Never again, he determined, would he lug the back-breaking buckets of sand to the villains who manned the kilns at Sanderson-Pilgrim Glass, Ltd. No more would those merciless masters have a chance to curse and cuff him if his sand buckets were delivered half empty. And never again would rude, uncouth bartenders at the pubs where he filched food have the opportunity to kick or beat him if they caught him stealing. "A pox on them all," he sniveled, hiding himself behind a thick, low iron post on the wharf to which mooring lines from a big frigate were attached. Making sure that he was well hidden behind the bollard, he peeped out to view the seething dock.

"Blimey," he muttered, "I *will* stow away. And I'll grow big and git to be a cabin boy. I'll scrub decks, clean pistols and cannons, and dump slop from the galley chutes. I'll take tankards of rum to the captain. Shine brass and cutlasses. But most of all, I will share in the ship's victuals." He sighed, rubbed his empty stomach, and scrooched down among the mooring lines, which looped loosely around the bollard. The boy yawned a great gape and immediately fell asleep. His hiding place was undiscovered. Darkness came on.

Perhaps it was the cold and damp which penetrated the pitiful tattered rags passing for his clothing that caused Ned to awake suddenly in the dark of the waterfront. Perhaps it was the ball of blazing light which passed over him and hung in the sky above the fog. Whatever the cause, Ned awoke. Only the lanterns of the various ships lying at dockside gave off any sign of light, and they were just yellow blobs in the thick fog that covered the area. Offshore, the deep, loud horns sounded their warning signals, reminding any and all that Bristol harbor was busy and full of seagoing vessels.

Like an eel, Ned slipped out of the loose coils of the manila hawser and furtively made his way through the fog. With the eyes of a cat, he dodged obstructions, barrels of merchandise, lumber, kegs of rum, and other cargo as he inched his way down the waterfront.

"Cawn't see nothing in this scummy fog," he fumed, wiping his nose on a tattered sleeve of his jerkin. "Got to find me a ship while it's still dark. Cawn't git caught trying to git aboard." He shivered, thinking of the consequences of stowing away—things he had heard the seafaring men talk about in the pubs. Sometimes stowaways were beaten and thrown overboard. Sometimes the ship's master marooned them. The boy was wise to the ways of the rough, sailing men; therefore, he was extremely careful now. He was determined to get aboard a ship before daylight appeared.

As he approached a group of warehouses down the dock, Ned espied the trim shape of a vessel. Here, also, lanterns hung about, and there was much activity around the ship. Men were loading or unloading a cargo.

Ned slipped behind a hogshead of tobacco and watched. The fog began to lift. The men were loading, he saw. His eyes took in the lines of the ship. He could tell that the deckhouses were cut down and that the gunwales were built up. He knew the reasons for these things, too. His young wisdom of the Bristol waterfront told him that this ship was a privateer. The deckhouses were nearly level with the decks so that the danger of flying wood splinters during battle would be lessened. The gunwales, or railings, along the sides were built up for protecting and concealing the crewmen on deck. Ned knew about privateers. To him, they represented next to the greatest adventure of the sea. The greatest being piracy.

"I'm going to stow on this vessel," Ned thought, suddenly making up his mind. When the ship would sail, where it was going, or what his own lot might be, Ned never gave a thought to at all. His busy mind and darting, appraising eyes now had only one problem: to get aboard unseen, find a hiding place, and stay put until the vessel was far out to sea.

And enterprising Ned Teach, nine years old, did just that! He even managed to secrete himself in a locker close to the galley.

There was a flat, bilge smell in the locker, and a penetrating odor of cheese, as if to ward off the smell of rats. There was also the odor of wet clothing and the polecat smells of unwashed men. All this medley was set off by a battery of noises overhead on deck. Ned realized the ship was getting ready to sail. Every timber resonated the shrieking of the rigging. Overhead, there were continual footfalls on the quarterdeck, and the clatter of ropes was deafening. The wooden sheathing of the vessel creaked, and suddenly, as she was probably entering the open Channel, the ship heeled into the force of the wind. Ned was buffeted around in the locker. It would take a while for the boy to acquire his sea legs.

For the first day or so, the odor of food from the galley and his great hunger nearly drove Ned wild. Then seasickness turned him into writhing misery.

That is when the ship's cook heard him and found Ned in the locker.

"By Drake's eyeballs! Ye filthy vermin," the one-armed cook swore, using his foot to roll Ned out. "Ye overgrown wharf rat, how did ye git into my galley?"

But Ned Teach was too seasick and miserable to move, much less answer. His black eyes seemed set in his sickly-green face. At the moment he would not have cared if the angry cook had tossed him into the sea with the sharks.

There had to be a decent streak hiding somewhere within the cook's makeup, because he took pity on Ned instead of reporting him as a stowaway. When Ned was able to eat, he gave him food. He gave him a bucket and some lye soap, instructing him to wash his filthy body.

"And scrub that mane of tangled black hair till ye're sure the vermin is gone. I want no more noxious animals in the galley that Hush Stiles runs. The rats are enough!"

After the bath in salt water and lye soap, the cook provided Ned with some hand-me-down clothing that was fairly clean and about ten sizes too big. Manila rope and twine helped to hold the clothes on him and provided some sort of a fit. For the first time that he could remember, Ned had a full belly.

Hush Stiles kept Ned in the galley, where he worked the boy hard. But Ned did not seem to mind at all, because in his rough way, the cook was kind to him and did not curse or beat him. Pretty soon, Ned Teach began to fill out and look more like a boy than a red-eyed wharf rat. If the captain of the privateer—the *Red Scorpion*—ever found out that Ned was a stowaway, nothing ever came of it. He stayed on the *Red Scorpion* long enough to graduate from the galley and become a cabin boy and, finally, a foremast hand on that privateer and many others which plied the seas between Europe, North America, and the Caribbean.

Being a foremast hand on privateers for more than twenty years taught Edward Teach a great deal about the lawlessness of privateering. Even though the privateer captains had been issued Letters of Marque by the English parliament—documents that authorized them to arm their ships with cannon, sign on fighting crews, and prey on the commerce of France and Spain during the wars of the Spanish Succession—Teach's sharp, appraising mind saw the practice for what it was—legalized piracy. And piracy *beyond the law*, without any doubt, lay dormant and fertile in the keen brain of Edward Teach during his years of privateer service. Not so dormant were his revengeful disposition and his streak of cruelty, which often wreaked near destruction and death on the hapless victims with whom he came in contact aboard ship or ashore in the taverns. The age itself, in which he had been born and come to manhood, was one when brutality was common and not thought exceptional. Certainly, the age offered few restrictions on the savage impulses which came to him. The rougher the sea life, the better he liked it; the bloodier the battle, the more he exulted. Many of his shipmates, on any vessel on which he served, shunned Teach like the plague. They knew that he had no respect for God nor man and believed that any ship under any flag, or any man weaker than he, was his own special prey to be dealt with as he saw fit.

Not a single ship's master ever raised Edward Teach to a command during his privateering years, and he built a bitter grudge against the captains. Each time the English vessels brought their captured prizes into port, where they were sold at auction, his burning ambition, to man his own ship—a real pirate ship—intensified. The intensity of this ambition did not abate when the wars ended. Edward Teach swore that he would never embark on the poorly paid and dull living of an ordinary seaman.

His obsessions made Teach more arrogant, more conniving, more cruel, and it was for these reasons that many captains got rid of him before he had served very long on their ships.

Captain James Stick was the skipper of the next-to-last English privateer on which Teach served. Stick very quickly formed a distrust of Teach. He abhorred his cruelty. He determined to rid himself of Teach. And there came a day in Kingston, Jamaica, when he did it.

For days, Teach had been roisterously mean-drunk. He had been so hatefully offensive to the other crewmen and arrogant toward Stick that the captain hunted him down in a Kingston pub and paid him off then and there.

Teach stood at the bar among a group of sailors. His lips curled in scorn, and his bulging black eyes leered in hate at the captain. Taking the bag of money the ship's master had handed him, Edward Teach hurled it on the bar of the pub.

"Drink up, mateys," he roared with a curse. "The pious captain has scuppered me. But he ain't heered the last of Ned Teach. Not by a dam'sight!" He grabbed a pistol from his bandolier and shot the floor between the captain's feet. A brass cap flew off the captain's boot and sailed over the bar into the rum bottles, breaking glass as it went.

The benumbed Captain Stick and the onlookers stood flabbergasted.

Teach replaced his smoking pistol, turned on his heel, and stalked out into the West Indies' night.

"Beach me, will he? One day I'll cut out his heart and roast it. Blast his bloody eyeballs! And I'll bet any swabby a ha'penny it won't be an hour afore I find me another berth!" His slovenly figure made its way down the beach toward another tavern.

Before dawn, in the black tropical night, the *Lily Wreath*, a privateer out of Bristol, sailed out of Jamaica with Edward Teach aboard.

As the last sail of the vessel flared to the breeze, fiery streaks of brilliance overhead illuminated the vessel. Abruptly, the streaks swirled into a bobbing ball of light, which traveled over the horizon, following the ship westward.

The complexity of Time's paradoxes was causing flicks on the edges of Corky's and Toby's awareness. Even though they were in a state of deep telesthesia, they knew that they were coexisting with Edward Teach at different points along a Time band. It did not seem odd at all that the brilliant Light and great Force were gearing Time to their minds or that their synapses were keyed by tensions they had never experienced. Their vision was clear as crystal—almost like second sight. Their awareness lay somewhere beyond, or within, the limits of thought. Their minds stayed in firm rapport. They had no awareness of their own physical bodies. It was as if they were invisible parts of something about which they would not concern themselves. Their cognizance now concerned their journey above the ship, which was sailing beneath them on the tropical waters that would soon open up into the broad Atlantic.

"We're observers of strange things in a fantastic situation," Corky telepathed.

"You can THINK that again," Toby sent back. "That ship beneath us is on its way to Bristol."

"And we'll be there before you can transmit 'Jack Robinson,'" Corky's Thought-force returned. "I wonder if we can sleep."

"The astronauts sleep in their space capsules," Toby transmitted. Corky's telepathy was silent. "If we're astronauts, we're funny-peculiar," Toby kept on transmitting. A rueful grin turned into a telepathic yawn. Toby's telepathy also became silent.

But there was still awareness between them—some sort of richness of sensory perception that made them know when the *Lily Wreath* docked at Bristol. Up above the fog, they watched the auction of the ship's cargo; they saw Teach lay on the cat-o'-nine-tails to a hapless seaman; they saw the privateer readied for another trip. It was as if their telepathy had now become supercharged. The bouncing ball of Light and its super Force held them glued as the *Lily Wreath* left Bristol harbor. High up, in the blue heavens, the Light followed the ship as it turned southward, heading again for the tropics.

CHAPTER SIX

THE GREAT Light-force carried Corky and Toby steadily southward, following the course of the *Lily Wreath*. Thought transference constantly passed between the young people like invisible dots and dashes from invisible radio operators.

"Numero Uno. Time Shuttle," Toby transmitted.

"Roger," Corky telepathed back. "By some inexplicable, phenomenal quirk of fate, we have been hurled backwards to the days of Edward Teach—a Time when a day is like ten thousand miles, when an hour is like a nanosecond, and a year is a different century."

"And Teach's Light is doing it all. Teach's Light is the Time Gate, the Time Lock, the Time Shuttle!" Toby telepathed. "Wowie!!!! What a journey!!!!"

Corky's telepathy picked up the exclamation marks and added a few of her own.

Whatever its trajectory, whatever its source of power —magnesium isotopes or whatever—Teach's Light, its pure radiance unhampered, was now whirling Corky and Toby not *backward* but *forward* in Time, sending them zooming over the Bahamas of the early eighteenth century.

The earth, which had seemed to fall so far away from them, appeared now to rise up to meet them. Their perception registered the gentle thunder of the billows striking the gleaming sands of a beach. Their intellects translated the images.

As usual, when it was coming to rest, the intense brilliance dimmed. The Light placed them high above a grove of sentinel palms on the dockside of New Providence harbor. As always, the centripetal force held them in a state of nearly suspended animation. The vantage point was splendid.

From their position, on that sun-sprinkled, tropical afternoon, Toby and Corky watched the *Lily Wreath* put into New Providence, where it took on water, food, barrels of rum, hundreds of bolts of silk, and more than fifty slaves.

Queen Anne's War had been over for three years, so there was no excuse for the English to plunder the ships of France and Spain. However, some of the more delinquent privateers had turned to smuggling; some, to pure piracy. The West Indies became the hotbed of both smuggling and piracy, and New Providence became the cesspool of the western hemisphere. The very scrapings of humanity walked its thoroughfares and frequented its dives. The shabby crew of the *Lily Wreath* added their share of squalidness to the prevailing riffraff already in port.

When the privateer was fully laden and all the slaves had been chained in the stinking hold, she set sail.

But there was one of the crewmen who did not board the vessel. There was one who *jumped* ship.

At the moment, that particular weathered roughie stood at the bar in Dimple's Tavern. He was a startling, striking figure. He had a beard which was coal black and very long. This evening, he wore his beard in twisted pigtails tied with ribbons, with some strands thrown back over his ears. The rest swept below his belt buckle. His clothes were black, and a floppy ebon hat perched on his bushy head of black hair. The heels of his black knee boots thwacked the barroom floor as he swaggered toward a table. His chest was festooned with pistol sashes, plus a bandolier which held three braces of pistols. An assortment of knives stuck out of his belt, and a poniard was stuck in the top of one boot leg. A wicked-looking cutlass swung at his side. The strangest part of his appearance was the long sulphur matches sticking out all around his face under the brim of the floppy black hat. In his hands he held large flagons of rum. Drinking from first one and then the other, he belched gustily, the raw spirits trickling from the corners of his mouth down into his matted beard. The merrymakers cast dour looks toward the man, but they left him strictly alone.

The door of the pub opened. A tall man, resplendent in a maroon velvet suit adorned by silver buttons, stepped in. Swinging at his side was a shining sword. The bandolier across his chest carried two pearl-handled pistols. A green velvet tricorne with a tall feather sat on his head. Long ringlets of red hair fell to his shoulders. His red beard was neatly trimmed. His boots were polished to a high sheen. A black eye patch covered his left eye. He stood inside the door—big and tough-looking—and surveyed the habitants of the pub.

Suddenly the roisterers let out a strident roar of welcome.

"By Beelzebub's backside!" an old salt bawled out. "Effen it ain't Captain Benjamin Hornigold hisself."

"Bartender, break out the grog," the merry crowd yelled. They lifted their tankards in a salute to Hornigold —one of the most famous and celebrated pirate captains in the Caribbean.

The man in black seethed in angry resentment at the adoration the seafarers showed Hornigold. Envy burned deeply within him, but he did not show it by even the flicker of an eyelid. He did not join in the toast. Instead, he spat out a mouthful of rum directly into the face of an unsuspecting sailor who stood by him.

"Gadszooks!" the seaman spluttered, wiping the grog from his face. "What did ye do that fer?"

The only answer he received was a disdainful sneer which curled the lips of the offender.

Hornigold raised his hand in recognition of the salute paid him by the crowd. Then he walked over to the man in black. Placing his arms akimbo, and facing him eyeball to eyeball, he addressed the other in a loud, haughty manner:

"Ned Teach, I would have words with ye. Now. Outside this den of screeching hellions."

"The name is BLACKBEARD, Hornigold! And I'll thankee to remember it." So saying, he set down his tankards and, rubbing his hands briskly around his hat brim, he set off the ring of sulphur matches in a popping, blazing inferno. Then, with a sweep of the floppy hat, he sent the stinking, fiery matches scattering to the floor and bouncing against the palm-thatched walls of the tavern, setting small fires wherever they landed.

"Scum!" the pockmarked bartender screamed at Blackbeard, flailing his dirty bar rag to try to beat out the flames. "Ye slimy, rum-punched son of Satan. Ye'll burn me tavern to smithereens!"

Like the strike of an asp, Blackbeard drew a pistol from his sash and neatly shot off the bartender's left ear. "Avast!" he thundered. "Another word," he snarled, "and ye'll git an ounce of lead in yer belly."

Hornigold snorted contemptuously at the situation and arrogantly made his way to the outside. Blackbeard followed. As he came to the door, he turned and, in a voice like a rumble of thunder capable of shaking the distant horizon, he bellowed at the stricken bartender:

"Think twicet afore ye try to insult Blackbeard, ye bilge-sucking scum. Even the cats and dogs, birds, and other varmits that has premonition flee when Blackbeard puts ashore." With that parting advice, he snatched a brace of pistols from his bandolier and let off a volley straight down the bar, shattering ale mugs, breaking bottles, and scattering thunderstruck seamen to the four winds.

Hornigold stood outside, waiting. There was not the slightest bit of fear about the captain. His air was one of insulting coolness. As he had stood before Blackbeard in the tavern, arms akimbo, so he stood now.

"What would the great Ben Hornigold want with me?" Blackbeard asked insolently, staring overbearingly at the captain.

"I hear ye're mightily wanting to become a gentleman of fortune," Hornigold answered, grinning facetiously. "Yer comportment jest now was certainly audacious enough. Well, how's about signing on with me? The *hunting*'s quite good, and New Providence is a pearl fer it. I hear some big things about ye, Ned Teach." Blackbeard glowered. " 'Scuse me," Hornigold corrected, grinning. "I fergot that ye called yerself Blackbeard now. And well ye might." He chuckled evilly, eyeing the mass of tangled black beard and hair. "Anyways, ye seem headed in the right direction: from a stowaway to cabin boy to privateer ain't a bad record. Scuttlebutt has it that ye're a real hellion on the privateers. Hear tell that many of the ships' masters git rid of ye 'cause ye're so feisty."

Blackbeard's eyes flashed murder.

Hornigold laid his hand on Blackbeard's shoulder and went on. "I can use a man like ye—one who ain't afeerd to lay 'em athwart or do a bit of keelhauling now and then. Lay yer course with me, matey. Point windward and we'll ride in fine carriages down the London streets," Hornigold ended braggingly.

"More likely we'd wind up like the brisk lads drying in the sun at Execution Dock," Blackbeard snorted. "Split me timbers," he said, pulling at his dirty beard, "I'd have to have a sick heart to sail with the likes of ye."

" 'Tain't many of me lads ever comes up to Old Bailey or Newgate," Hornigold said. "And none ain't been hanged like a dog and sun-dried on the docks of London, either," he said, angrily.

Blackbeard began strutting up and down the board-walk in front of the tavern. His scheming mind was working like a well-oiled clock. But he was determined not to show his great interest to Hornigold. "It's the chance I've been waiting fer," he thought to himself. "I'll sign up with Hornigold, and use me energy and cunning." He rolled his quid over his tongue. "And me-thinks I'll have a ship of me own a lot quicker than old Hornigold knows." He kept walking. Hornigold kept pace.

" 'Tis the glory of the sea. And of battle, Blackbeard," Hornigold said. "I have plenty fer rum and a good fling whenever I want 'em. Then to sea again when the days git boring. And I puts some away—some here, some there —and none too much in any one place, by reason of suspicion. Ye may lay to that."

"Jest the life to suit the temper of a good Englisher like meself," Blackbeard said, roaring with laughter. Suddenly he envisioned a cat-o'-nine-tails or a belaying pin in his big hands. A recollection of some of the privateer captains who had scuppered him also flashed through his mind. Circumstances for revenge had never been better. But the biggest item on his mind was that this just might be the opportunity to get his hands on a ship that he could call his own. Suddenly he stopped pacing, turned, and faced Hornigold.

"By the blood of me blooming eyeballs, I'll jine ye!" he said, laughing raucously.

"And I'll stand ye a double grog to seal the bargain," Hornigold told him, giving him a thwack between the shoulders.

So, a devil's pact was agreed upon, and Edward Teach, alias Blackbeard, sailed from New Providence aboard Benjamin Hornigold's pirate ship.

As he had determined he would do through energy and cunning, Blackbeard soon exhibited his marksman's eye, his ability at dirty infighting, and a thirst for blood unmatched by any pirate of his time. Hornigold was quick to recognize these qualities and, for a while, he liked them and all went well. He made Blackbeard his protégé and lieutenant. If the veteran crewmen of Hornigold's ship resented the attention given the newcomer, they knew better than to protest.

The pirates sailed up and down the North American coast on plundering expeditions and, after careening their ship in Virginia, they began their long voyage back to the West Indies, plundering and killing as they went.

On their way south, they captured a French Guinea ship. Long boats were put out and, very shortly, the French merchantman was seething with murderous, looting pirates. Needless to say, Blackbeard was one of the first to board the ship. His deadly pistols and cutlass made horrible inroads among the hapless crew.

Blackbeard's piercing, appraising eyes went everywhere, looking the ship over from stem to stern. He noted her trim lines, her spritsails and sprit topsails and flying jib. "A lusty ship," he said to himself, not missing an item of the well-built vessel. His past experience told him that she was maneuverable and very fast. At last, he thought, here was a vessel that offered the means for realizing his ambitions to have his own ship. He was determined, by some hook or crook, that the captured prize should become his own.

When Hornigold divvied up the booty with the crew, Blackbeard took none of it. Instead, he demanded the French Guineaman as his prize. There was no argument. More and more of late both Hornigold and the crew had come to dislike and distrust Blackbeard—even to despise and fear him. Giving him the captured ship seemed to Hornigold an ideal way to rid himself of the obnoxious Edward Teach.

So, at last, Blackbeard acquired his own ship. With a handful of the more dissident members of Hornigold's crew, Blackbeard manned the prize and set off on a cruise of his own, in the general direction of the Windward Islands.

Hornigold returned with his sloop to New Providence, where, at the arrival of Captain Woodes Rogers, the governor, he accepted the King's offer of clemency to all pirates who would give up their evil trade. From that time on, till his death, Hornigold devoted his resources to helping the governor of New Providence rid the Caribbean of the piracy that infested it.

The pirate grapevine spread the word about Hornigold's defection and about the King's offer of pardon. Down in the Windward Islands, Blackbeard heard about it. He snorted in derision. He had no notion of accepting any pardon or giving up his ship or his pirating. He felt that his days of glory were just beginning. But he made a mental note to avoid the Caribbean territory patrolled by Woodes Rogers' pirate-hunters.

Teach and his crew busily applied themselves to outfitting his prize as a first-class pirate ship. It was not long before forty cannons thrust their ugly muzzles through the gunports. New ensigns of the skull and crossbones and the hourglass with flaming arrow replaced the French flag. They flew flamboyantly from the tallest mast. With a gallon of rum, Teach baptized his vessel *Queen Anne's Revenge*, in ironical patriotism for the late ruler of England.

The chains which held the gunports open on the *Anne* were polished to gleaming brightness by the motley gun crew. The cannon gleamed above gun decks that were painted red. Teach worked his men like demons. The metal work and rigging shone. Even the stained glass windows of the poop deck were washed and polished.

Blackbeard's quarters contained mullioned and tinted glass windows, which looked over a small veranda over the rudder. The ceiling was gold and white. Heavy purple, brocaded curtains hung from ceiling to floor. There was a low, black, French-woodwork bed, ornately carved with nymphs and cupids. Across it, messily laid, was a coverlet of red and silver. Several sea chests lined the walls. Some were open, and their contents of fine linens and expensive wearing apparel for both men and women spilled out.

The *Queen Anne's Revenge* might not keep her trim, rich appearance very long, because of the slatternly habits of Teach and his crew, but at the moment, Blackbeard felt himself to be a monarch among the Brotherhood of pirates.

"The *Anne's* got fire power, me hearties. And swift as a hornet she be," Blackbeard gloated to the pirate crew he had gathered in the tropics. "What sez ye, Hush

Stiles?" He pointed to a one-armed man standing near him. The stump of Stiles' other arm was outfitted with a wicked-looking hook. Stiles raised the hook and saluted his captain. "The Devil sure guided ye to me a SECOND time, old matey," Blackbeard went on. "I now baptize ye chief cook of the *Anne's* galley—a galley that's a blasted sight better than the one ye once had on the *Red Scorpion*. I order ye never to be stingy with the hardtack, the bear bacon, or gulls' eggs!" With that admonition, Blackbeard dashed a flagon of rum over Hush Stiles—the same cook who had befriended him when he was a nine-year-old stowaway.

Stiles grinned lopsidedly, shook himself like a Labrador, and skulked off to the galley.

"Now, let's git flapping!" Blackbeard roared out the orders. "Lively, ye swab," the pirate bellowed, singling out a wizened sea thief standing by and dealing him a clout in the face. The ruffian grinned bloodily, spitting out two of his teeth on the deck—his only protest. Blackbeard laughed in satanic delight.

The crew manned their stations. It was not long before the *Anne* was out of the harbor and was striking a course which carried her to the Atlantic sea lanes of international shipping.

Up above, Teach's Light tilted and seemed to climb. It began its rhythmic bobbing, as if it were keeping time with the movement of the ocean below. The super brilliance seemed to have an inertial guidance system. The bobbing had no effect on its precise operation or direction—a direction that followed whatever path Blackbeard took on land or sea. In all the universe around them, it seemed to Corky and Toby that there was no actual light except Teach's Light, unless they counted the faint luminosity away, away down which separated into streaks of phosphorescence given off by the curling tips of the rolling waves. Teach's Light carried Toby and Corky with a sort of unholy purposefulness—the same purposefulness they knew was seething in the personality of Blackbeard who, this very second, was sailing on the *Queen Anne's Revenge* beneath them.

CHAPTER SEVEN

Let's vary piracee
With a little burglaree.
—W. S. GILBERT
The Pirates of Penzance

THE ANTECHAMBERS OF Toby's brain were tolerating thought forces almost too great for comprehension. Corky was registering them all.

"Holy cow!" Toby wailed. "I feel older than Methuselah."

"Don't knock it," Corky sent back. "Even though it's a real mind-bender, we seem to be growing up pretty fast."

"But how in the dickens can we do this? Follow Blackbeard all over the face of the map in the eighteenth century? We're of the TWENTIETH CENTURY!" Toby thought, his state of telesthesia nearly sending out sparks.

Somewhere in the deep stirrings of the medulla, Corky's Thought-force transmitted:

"Well, Mister, who's to blame for all this? Whose insatiable curiosity was it to find the source of Teach's Light? Who can tell us how we were flung into this maelstrom of Time?" It was just a gentle reminder, no rebuke.

Toby recognized the mind-staggering truth of Corky's transmission. *He* had been the nagging one, always egging her on to help him search for the elusive Light. He still felt the same stubborn determination. "Well, by darn, we're getting a real bird's-eye view of Blackbeard," his telepathy affirmed.

"Roger," Corky transmitted. "And a bird's-eye view of tropical islands and whirling Space and Time."

The time was early 1717. The *Queen Anne's Revenge* was nearing St. Vincent in the Windward Islands. The *Great Allen*, a large British merchantman loaded with valuable cargo, hove into sight. Blackbeard and his crew took the vessel without a fight. Captain Taylor, of the *Great Allen*, and his men were set ashore. After the pirates had transferred the valuables to the *Anne*, they set the captured ship on fire. The *Allen* blazed until the fire gutted the hull to the waterline.

The news of the fate of the *Great Allen* spread. HMS *Scarborough*, a thirty-gun British warship, put out to sea in search of Blackbeard and his vessel.

For days, the weather held. Under a blue sky the *Queen Anne's Revenge* sailed through brisk gales and then gentle breezes when the freshening winds abated. The ocean seemed bereft of other vessels. It had been three or four days since the pirates had espied even a distant sail. The crew doggedly attended their shipside chores. But, in all of them, there was building up a tension which started mutterings of impatience and discontent.

Blackbeard itched for action. To ward off some of the boredom, he spent his waking hours swilling black rum. His state, in anyone else, would have approached a drunken catalepsy. At the touch of a mood, he would explode into maudlin wrath or mad laughter. Yet, he kept his wits about him.

Suddenly, the lookout's cry smote his ear.

"Deck ahoy! Frigate-man-o'-war!" the foremast lookout screeched. "Looks like the *Scarborough!*"

Teach snatched up his long glass, gripped its leather sling in his teeth, and rapidly started climbing the quarter rigging.

"By Satan's drawers!" he bellowed. "It is the *Scarborough!*"

From the quarter mast, his great voice boomed down commands as he descended to the deck.

"Git round shot heated—hotter than Hell itself," he bawled to his chief gunner, Israel Hands.

Israel Hands gaped with astonishment. "Gadszooks! Ye ain't going to fight *her*, are ye, Cap'n? That's a British man-o'-war!"

"Shut yer mincing gob of argument afore I stave me boot in it, Israel Hands. By Satan's breath, we will fight her. I am sick unto death of running like a cur from that damned Britisher. Now git a move on afore I pelt out yer eyeballs with me pistols or give ye a taste of this waist dagger dipped in Madagascar poison!"

For the next thirty minutes, men who had seemed too

bored or too besotted with rum to move now galvanized into action. Gun crews packed hammocks, bedding, and seabags into the nets that covered their cannon stations to ward off the deadly splinters which they knew would fly in battle. Powder and cartridges were brought up from the magazines in leather-covered budge barrels and stowed well away from the cannon. Tubs of water, with bedding soaked in them, were placed between the guns. Other tubs filled with vinegar water were set beside the cannons for sponging purposes. Teach's tongue lashed out at all, goading his pirate crew to a peak of fighting frenzy. It was no common occurrence for a pirate ship to engage a man-of-war. The pirate captain was determined to be prepared.

The boatswain and his men furled the light sails and brought them to the deck. The doors to the powder magazines were hung with wet blankets to fend off any spark.

By the direction taken by the topsails of the *Scarborough*, Teach saw the warship alter its course toward the *Queen Anne's Revenge*. He grinned diabolically, as he cast his eyes about over the deck. He saw the leather buckets of blue, explosive powder, the canvas slings of heavy shot, the gun braziers that held seething-hot incandescent cannon balls, the long muskets, cartridges, wads, and ramming irons. He saw his crew armed to the teeth with cutlasses, dirks, pistols, and poniards. He looked down at his own body armament. His evil grin showed satisfaction.

"Be gawd, I'm ready fer her," he bellowed.

"We got time to turn afore the wind and run, Cap'n. We got a fair chance to git away," Israel Hands said, firmly believing that Teach had gone mad.

"Stop mewling around like a blasted leper, Israel Hands!" Teach roared out a blasphemous oath. "I said I weren't running from that frigate. Git them gunnery grummets a-running with them tubs of vinegar water and have them wash down the woodwork inside with alum water." He brandished his cutlass at the half-naked men running with slopping tubs through the between-deck passages. "Chips," he bawled at the carpenter, "git them sheets of lead and wads of oakum. Stand ready to plug shot holes. Satan blister me if I don't singe the King's beard this day!" His laughter echoed and re-echoed throughout the ship.

The *Scarborough* bore down. The pirates on the *Anne* frantically knotted up the canvas waistcloth on the man-height screens that protected them from grapeshot.

"Avast!" Teach yelled. A sudden, harebrained scheme had hit him. He was determined to carry it out. "Every man below. Unbolt them gunports, Israel Hands, and don't let ary a flap fall open. Chock back the muzzles of them cannons level to the gun'ls."

The gunner stood like one paralyzed. He was certain

now that Captain Teach had gone as mad as a lamprey eel in frigid waters.

"God's breath, Cap'n," Israel Hands wheezed out. "No marksman in the rigging? No mortar-throwers?"

"Ye writhing lugworm," Teach snarled. "Do ye want me to slice ye into skilly? Do as I say! Devil take me fer all yer arguments, and Satan blister yer tongue fer running yer fat gob. That's a British warship, matey. She'll not fire on an unmanned vessel!"

Israel Hands backed off, knowing that what Teach had said was true.

"John Husk," Teach bawled. "Go to me cabin and open them sea chests of women's wearing apparel. Fetch out a wench's white gown and dress up in it. WHITE, I said, and dress like a lady, ye bilge-drowned rat. Now step lively, blast ye! Ye're going to be a ghost lady standing at the helm steering. Git that white flowing skirt we took from the Grandee's wife, and don't take no time to primp," he roared at the astounded man. Edward Teach shook with satanic delight.

John Husk ran through the between-decks, agreeing full well with Israel Hands that the waiting Blackbeard had gone stark, raving crazy. He threw open sea chests until he finally found a long, white, full skirt and shirtwaist. Thrusting them over his pirate clothing in makeshift fashion, he darted back to Captain Teach.

"To the helm, ye sop-witted oaf!" Teach bellowed. "And give that shirtwaist and skirt full leeway to the wind. Cap'n Hume will swear he's seen ghosts afore this day is over. Too bad, John Husk, ye don't have me long black beard to blow agin all that whiteness," Teach said, roaring with laughter, as he viewed from cover the startling figure of his crewman, whose long red hair was swinging outward in the breeze.

Husk stood with legs braced wide. He had to, else his trembling, knocking knees would have thrown him his length. If the truth could have been told, Husk would not have been able to say of which he was more afraid— the British frigate bearing down or the demonic face of Edward Teach. The whipstaff helm in his hands bucked and throbbed from the pressures of the great seas that surged beneath the *Queen Anne's Revenge*.

The *Scarborough* drew nearer. Husk could see the ominous yellow and black stripes of the warship. "Like a bloody wasp!" he gulped.

The shrouds of the frigate shone white. Her gunports were open and purposeful-looking. Red-coated musketeers moved among the halyards and yardarms.

"Must be Grog Vernon piloting," Teach mumbled in his beard, fearing that his scheme was falling through.

The *Scarborough* fired its warning. Teach, crouched behind a hatch leewards of the frigate, grinned like a satyr as he saw the shot fall high and off the *Anne's* prow. He knew the frigate would fire again immediately, and it would be a well-aimed blow designed to partially disable the *Anne* so that the grappling hooks could fasten and so that a boarding party could set upon her like a pack of wolves.

The shot came. The *Anne* jerked. A mast snapped, and a jib sail hit the deck with a clatter.

"Hold her, matey. Hold her steady, ye Grandee's darling," Teach directed Husk. The pirate's great voice, now a harsh whisper, penetrated the hearing of a frantic John Husk, whose state of nerves caused the helm to jump in such a way that the prow of the frigate scrunched into the *Queen Anne's Revenge* with a splintering of timbers.

The *Anne* began to veer. "Now!" Teach thundered. "Fire the broadside, Israel Hands!"

From dozens of hiding places Teach's men scrambled. The square gunports of the *Anne* belched out their broadside—a successive firing from bow to stern of the cannon. The impact of the firings hurled John Husk against the lazaret hatch, where he lay unconscious and unheeded by his shipmates.

The *Scarborough* sent back a blast of gunfire which made the pirate ship shudder. Teach's men shrieked and cursed like demons. Their muskets boomed, and hand-made grenades burst their deadliness against the frigate. Again and again, Teach's gunners sent broadsides against the man-of-war. They had telling results. The *Scarborough* began to limp off.

"She's headed fer the nearest port in Barbados," Teach said. He laughed like a demon. The last the pirates saw of the *Scarborough* was the red flames in her bulwark.

"See them fires, mateys?" Teach asked, his harsh laughter ringing out over the waves as he sat down on the quarterdeck with his logbook. "That's the Devil's imps doing a ballet fer His Majesty. Break out the grog, me hearties, while I record fer all the world to see how this day Blackbeard has bested the King's navy!"

The celebration went on around him while Blackbeard laboriously wrote in his log. In the furor of the victory-crazed pirates, Tanzie Greene was tossed head first into a hogshead of molasses. Some of the pirates fell to with axes and burst open the barrel staves. Molasses and Tanzie came oozing out all over the deck. The molasses caught Blackbeard's boots.

"Avast, ye vermin!" the pirate squalled, bellowing with laughter at Tanzie's plight. "Throw him overboard and clean the deck down to the scuppers."

No sooner said than Tanzie was tossed over the side into the black waters. Blackbeard looked down at his labored writing and read what he had written in his uncertain script:

Sighted Scabrugh—*tricked her—John Husk at helm of our vessel dressed like ghost of Grandee's lady—all hands hiding, watching Cap'n Hume's confusion (Scratch that) Grog Vernon was piloting—Grog Vernon's confusion: sent volleys of great shot, small shot, prow and broadside: Scabrugh limped off towards Barbadoes: nine of Anne's rogues kilt—ten with wounds; tended to all with sail needle and hot tar; Stiles broke out galley store of rum in celebration; Tanzie so swashed, fell into molasses barrel and was tossed over the side fer being a petty annoyance—such a day.*

He closed the log and stood up. "Fetch me a gallon of spirits, Hush Stiles," he bellowed to the cook. "And trim them sails fer St. Kitts!"

"St. Kitts?" Toby's telepathy erupted. "Well, isn't that the kitten's britches and cat's pajamas!" But he felt that his attempt to be funny escaped Corky.

"Are we like the spirits in Dickens' *Christmas Carol?*" she thought. "There's some kind of aura about this crazy Light—some sort of pervasive quality that seems as if the fate of the world is centered in it—as if all decisions that control us and the universe flow out from it."

"And all it looked like from my front porch was a bobbing ball of light over Little Dismal," Toby's telepathy sputtered. "I think it must be a bodiless demon right out of the Devil's Hell!"

Corky's Thought-force emitted a fascinating giggling, which Toby's telesthesia registered but could not quite fathom. He had been dead serious. He had not meant to be funny that time.

Corky's ESP picked up Toby's discomfiture. The giggling emission stopped. "You're beginning to sound just like Blackbeard," she transmitted.

Under the brilliance of Teach's Light, a low-hanging, invisible moon dipped toward a horizon which did not show anywhere.

CHAPTER EIGHT

What else seest thou
In the dark, backward abysm of Time?
—SHAKESPEARE

L IKE a tesseract of incandescence—a spatial hypercube
of effulgent splendor—Teach's Light kept streaking
westward, holding Toby and Corky fast within its luminosity. Their thought transference remained sharp and
constant. Within each there seemed to have developed a
great yearning patience which, like a sixth sense, was
warning them that this backward-forward journey in
Time had not yet ended; that they must still be observers
until the saga of Blackbeard was played out to its end.
Their perceptions, therefore, registered an unimpas-
sioned expectancy at times, and at other times, a fearful
apprehension.

Perhaps there was some measure of hero worship and
respect for Blackbeard among his peers, but seamen on
legitimate vessels plying the waters of the Atlantic Ocean
felt mostly dread concerning the pirate. They swore that
the Devil and Blackbeard were blood brothers. The pirate liked the comparison and bragged that he *was* Satan's
brother. He missed no opportunity to demonstrate to
his crew that he was superior to them in every way.

One day, during a drunken frolic in a tavern, Blackbeard slipped a pistol under the table and shot his gunner, Israel Hands, in the knee.

In shock and pain, Hands raised his head from examining his shattered kneecap. "What did ye do that fer, Cap'n?" he asked mournfully.

"Iffen I didn't shoot one of ye now and then, ye'd fergit who I am," Blackbeard told him. "I'll doctor it fer ye." Whereupon he doused Israel's bleeding wound with a flagon of rum. For the rest of his days Israel Hands carried a crippled knee, which handicapped him greatly but did not cause him to give up pirating.

Blackbeard had to have excitement. He thrived on it. On dull days when there was no plundering, he had to make his own thrills—thrills which were usually tinged with cruelty and touched by terror. He firmly believed that such cruel displays were necessary to maintain discipline and keep down the frequent plots to remove him from his position of authority. To many around him, it just seemed that Blackbeard *enjoyed* being mean as sin.

There came one day when the *Queen Anne's Revenge* was becalmed on a glassy sea. There was not a breath of breeze to stir the limp sails hanging from the yardarms. The pirate was bored and his crew were irritable and spoiling for a fight. For the lack of something to do, some of the men started to break open the rum barrels.

"Blast yer eyeballs, ye shirking lubbers," Blackbeard bawled at them. "Iffen it's fer something to do, I'll make it hot enough fer ye!" He stood up and his gimlet eyes bored a hole through them. "I'll make a real Hell fer ye, and we'll see how long ye can bear that. And I'm calling fer volunteers, mateys. So, some of ye swabbies step right up!" He brandished his cutlass through the air, and crewmen ducked out of the way. Three of the pirates accepted Blackbeard's challenge and followed him down into the hold of the ship. Like a friendly dog, Hush Stiles tagged along behind. They all sat down on the ballast stones.

"Bring me seven pots of sulphur, John Gills," Blackbeard commanded. "Shet them hatches tight, Joe Curtis. Now, light up them pots, John Husk. We'll soon see how the Devil lives when he gits lonesome." Blackbeard shook with laughter, grabbing Stiles by his arm-hook, lifting him, and turning him around like a spin-button. "Damnation seize me soul," he chortled, "I'll not give none of ye quarter ner take no quarter from ye!" So saying, he plopped himself down on the ballast stones by the others.

The dark hold of the *Queen Anne's Revenge* was soon filled with swirling clouds of choking sulphur fumes and smoke. The three volunteers and Hush Stiles began screaming for fresh air.

"This is Hell on earth!" they bawled. "The Cap'n is as mad as a lamprey." They lunged crazily, clawing at their throats for breath.

Only then did Blackbeard order the hatches thrown

open. "A-ha, ye sniveling wretches," he thundered, "ye saw it was *me* who held out the longest. And ye may lay to that!"

"Aye, Cap'n, ye held out," John Gills croaked. "But ye must have the gills of Beelzebub. Even yerself has got a tinge of Gallows Green about ye."

"Me lad," Blackbeard said, grinning satanically, "ye've jest give me a brilliant idee. Next time ye varmits git restless, we'll play at Gallows. Then we'll see who can swing longest from the gibbet without gitting throttled."

"Shrive me soul," John Gills lamented. "I can already feel the rope at me neck!"

"Ye'll feel that noose sooner than ye think, iffen ye don't attend to yer knittin'," Blackbeard swore at them all, as they scrambled out of the hold.

"Freshening breeze!" the lookout yelled.

"Be gaw, it is!" Blackbeard acknowledged. "Bos'n, git them sails up. Everybody git crackin'. We're sailing! Maybe this time we'll git all the way to Bath Town in the Carolina Province. It's about time," he mumbled, "that I take advantage of some of that safety the governor's secretary hinted at and some of them warehouses he promised for storage. Why, I might even accept the King's pardon that the governor is offering, marry me a new bride, and settle down in Bath Town like the English gentleman I am!" He guffawed at the idea. On second thought, the notion did not seem too farfetched at all. But there was a long sail ahead. There was plenty of time—plenty of time for his devious mind to lay all kinds of plans.

Somewhere close to Honduras, in Spanish America, Stede Bonnet, the "gentleman" pirate, who had found his life so dull and himself so henpecked that he had out-fitted a trim ship called the *Revenge* and had taken up pirating to escape boredom, ran across Blackbeard. The ships were anchored off Turniff about ten leagues from the Bay of Honduras. Blackbeard's appraising eyes took in the trim lines of Bonnet's vessel, and his covetous, scheming mind began to churn with ideas. When Bonnet appeared alongside in a short boat, Blackbeard welcomed him aboard the *Anne*. Major Bonnet had come, believing that Blackbeard could teach him much about pirating.

And Blackbeard did!

But to his later sorrow, Bonnet did not get taught in the way that he had anticipated.

Blackbeard determined to acquire Bonnet's *Revenge*. His cunning mind showed him just how to do it, clever "con" man that he was. He hinted and insinuated strong-ly that Bonnet knew so little of maritime life that it would be best if Major Bonnet joined him on the *Anne*.

"Ye can take it easy from the cares and fatigues of sea voyages till ye learn the ins and outs, Major," Blackbeard told him, ingratiatingly.

Bonnet listened and was taken in by Blackbeard's smooth talk.

"I'll even put a man from me crew on the *Revenge* as

cap'n," Blackbeard went on, "with yer consent, of course, and ye can stay aboard the *Anne* and learn yer fill about pirating and maritime tricks."

Bonnet consented. And wily Blackbeard, without one speck of trouble, acquired himself another pirate ship. He immediately named one of his crew, a man called Richards, to be the new captain of Bonnet's sloop.

While the pirates were still anchored off Turniff, they espied a sloop coming in. Richards, on the *Revenge*, probably with orders from Blackbeard, slipped his cable and ran out to meet the sloop. Up went the black pirate flag on the *Revenge*. The sloop *Adventure*, out of Jamaica, with David Harriot as master, struck sail and came to, nearly under the stern of Blackbeard's ship. The crew from the Jamaican vessel were hustled aboard the *Anne*, and Blackbeard put some of his own crew under Israel Hands to man the *Adventure*—a prize which under the pirate code rightfully belonged to Stede Bonnet. Little by little, Major Bonnet began to realize his folly in being so taken in by Blackbeard.

When the band weighed from Turniff in the early spring of 1717, Bonnet was on the *Anne* with Blackbeard. Richards stayed on the *Revenge*, and Hands manned the *Adventure*. In the Bay of Honduras they captured a large ship and four sloops out of Jamaica and Boston. Up and down Spanish America they hunted and captured prizes. Bonnet became more and more melancholy about his shortsightedness. He began to see that

Blackbeard could not be trusted to obey the laws of piracy. Hatred began to build within him.

Up and down the Atlantic coast the pirate band plagued shipping. One day during the summer, they captured a leaky sloop out of Antigua, bound for Philadelphia, loaded with rum, molasses, sugar, cotton, indigo, and about twenty-five pounds in money. Toward the end of July, after selling and dividing up the loot, Bonnet manned the sloop with a small crew and set sail toward the Cape Fear River. He named his sloop the *Royal James*. It was a far cry from having his trim vessel *Revenge*, but he knew it was useless to try to get her back from Edward Teach. "Gentleman" Stede did not relish any more of Blackbeard.

As for Blackbeard, he had got what *he* wanted. For Bonnet, he felt only contempt. He chortled secretly, thinking what a big joke it had been to palm off on "that bloody fop" the *Royal James*, which was so leaky that he would be surprised if she did not sink under the dandified legs of Bonnet before he reached Wilmington!

Down the coast, toward Charles Town, Teach sailed with his band, taking a brigantine and two sloops on the way. Off the bar at Charles Town, they took a ship bound for London. The next day they took another vessel coming out of the harbor and two vessels going in, besides another brigantine lying in the harbor with fourteen Negroes aboard. Several ships lay at sail, ready to go out to sea, but none dared to venture. The incoming vessels found themselves in the same predicament. Blackbeard totally interrupted the trade of flourishing Charles Town harbor. It was a situation to his liking. To the people in the southern province, it was disaster. They had not yet recovered from a recent, terrible Indian war when the pirates infested them.

To make matters worse, some perverse streak in Blackbeard caused him to issue an ultimatum to the town that he must have a chest of medicine. He would send three of his pirates after the chest, and if his demands were not met immediately, he would murder all the prisoners from Charles Town he had taken, send up their heads to the governor, and set on fire the ships he had seized.

"That'll git the vermin moving!" Blackbeard bragged.

"But why didn't ye demand gold, Cap'n?" a wizened sea dog made so bold as to inquire. "Why a medicine chest? Ain't we got plenty of laudanum?"

"Shet yer fop," Blackbeard hissed, backhanding the hapless man. "Iffen I says I want medicine, that's how bloody well it is, and be-dam'd to ye fer curiousness!"

The chastened sailor slunk off out of Blackbeard's reach, only too happy to have got off so lightly.

For fear of bringing more calamities upon themselves, the people of Charles Town got together the chest of medicine and sent it to Blackbeard.

Among the prisoners he had taken was Samuel Wragg,

one of the members of the town council. When Blackbeard found out this man's importance, he raised his demands. The town came across, and this time Blackbeard indulged in no bloodletting. He and his crew sailed out of Charles Town with a medicine chest worth between three and four hundred pounds and gold and sterling silver worth nearly fifteen hundred pounds, which they had blackmailed out of the natives of Charles Town.

From Charles Town, Blackbeard set sail for the north province of Carolina. At no time in his life had the pirate been so bloated with his own importance. At no time in his life had he ever felt so rich and powerful. But nagging worry set in. He distrusted many of his crewmen. He had trained them, had he not? He knew just how their minds worked. He knew that he was a constant target, and that if he let down his guard for an instant, some of them would take advantage. Another thing Blackbeard could not abide was seeing the captured booty going to so many other than himself and his own chosen friends. So, again, he put his clever mind to work.

"By Satan's drawers," he swore, "I'll break up the Company and secure the money and best effects fer me-self," he vowed. "Jest as simple as that, be gaw!"

So, in early September, while at Beaufort Inlet on the pretext of careening his ships, he and his picked cohorts grounded the *Revenge* and deliberately wrecked and sank his flagship, the *Queen Anne's Revenge*, his brig, the *Flame*, and the *Adventure*. This accomplished, Black-beard, with forty of his trusted cronies, transferred the bulk of the loot to a sloop, which they had previously used as a tender. The pirate and his chosen crew boarded the sloop. From the grounded and wrecked vessels he took seventeen of the troublesome pirates and marooned them on an island about a league from the mainland—an island where there were no birds, animals, vegetation, or water to sustain them—an island of nothing but bare sand.

News flew fast on the pirate grapevine. Blackbeard was guilty of breaching his own code. Blackbeard was a dangerous, treacherous villain among his peers!

But again, Blackbeard did not care what people thought about him. When he sailed into Bath Town, one of the first things he did was to take twenty of his men, march up to the Governor's Palace, and accept His Majesty's Proclamation of Pardon for Pirates. This time around, he felt sure that he would have the governor on his side. Blackbeard knew how to "sweeten the pot" by distributing fine gifts in places where they counted most. He already felt that he had the governor's secretary in his keg-top-sized hands.

Once he was established in Bath, it was not long before many of the townspeople began to dread Blackbeard like a plague among them. Their grudging acceptance of the pirate was based on their fear and on the rumors that the governor seemed to tolerate every wicked thing that

Blackbeard perpetrated. When the pirate walked the thoroughfares, they were repelled by his dirty, slovenly appearance and his drunken, swearing obscenities.

But this repulsive creature had a chink in his armor—young women!

In spite of his bluster and bragging, in spite of his slovenly appearance, many women were struck with romantic notions about the swashbuckling corsair. Blackbeard became maudlin with infatuation for every harbor girl that struck his fancy. He firmly believed in marriage.

And he married fourteen women!

In Bath Town, everybody whispered about his fourteenth and last marriage to Prudence Lutrelle, daughter of a Bath widow. The young lady was barely sixteen, fragile and slight, with great dark eyes and a dark complexion, and was a great favorite of Governor Eden. Governor Eden married the couple, and people whispered that he was forced to do so against his will because Blackbeard held blackmailing threats over the governor's head. This rumor was never proved, but after this marriage, Blackbeard got cockier than ever. He boasted and bragged that he could now be invited into any home in Carolina. At first, the pirate entertained the planters on a lavish scale, but it was not long before the marriage palled and Blackbeard found his fortune diminished. After a few weeks of pretense, he threw off his mask of hypocrisy and openly slipped back into his old ways as a full-fledged pirate. If possible, he became even more hated and feared by all the people of the Carolina coast, who now became sure that Blackbeard was the very worst of all his pirate kind. Merchant ships feared to venture upon the sea. Trade was almost entirely cut off from all the coastal towns.

One day Blackbeard anchored off the mouth of Bath Creek. The pirate and a handful of his men loaded a longboat and rowed shoreward toward Eden's Palace. On the shore, the governor's secretary and one or two aides awaited him near the mouth of the tunnel, which was rumored to run directly to the Palace.

"Sugar and cocoa to sweeten yer gullet, and give some to the Governor," Blackbeard bellowed, as he swung ashore. The crew unloaded the bags of sugar along with some bolts of silk, a chest of spices, and a very small sea chest which contained a few pieces of eight.

"Did you find all this on a captured prize, Captain?" one of the aides asked piously.

"Shiver me timbers iffen any of it was took off a captured prize," Blackbeard returned savagely. "I *discovered* an abandoned vessel on the high seas. She was all awreck and listing to port. Not a human scalawag aboard her— jest a tomcat. That, me hearty, is legitimate salvaged cargo. Now ain't that so, Caesar?" Blackbeard addressed a huge black pirate standing near.

"Lud gaw, hit's de truuf, Cap'n," the Negro swore, rolling his eyes heavenward and crossing himself religiously.

Blackbeard grabbed a sack of sugar. He drew his poniard from his boot top and made a slash in the cloth bag. Then, grabbing the sack of sugar, he upended it—all one hundred weight of it—over Caesar's woolly head. The big black gasped for breath, spitting and blowing sugar every-which-a-way.

"Now ye're baptized the *sweetest* villain this side of the Pearly Gates," Blackbeard told him, howling with fiendish laughter. "Now start toting the booty down this tunnel afore I cut off them big jackass ears of yours. Git!"

Suddenly, and lasting only a second or two, a brilliant, nearly blinding stream of light flashed over Archbell's Point and into the tunnel. It seemed to paralyze everybody except Blackbeard.

"Never fear, me hearties," Blackbeard guffawed. "That's only the Devil lighting me way!"

The flick-flick-flicks of anger in Toby's brain waves were crisp and incisive. They almost seemed to hit the walls of the tunnel with rhythmic, infinitesimal muffled vibrations. His sensors picked up Corky's giggling telepathy, but the fury that had mounted in Toby's synapses could not appreciate Corky's levity.

"That old rapscallion called US the DEVIL!" his Thought-force raged. "Why are you giggling?"

" 'Sticks and stones may break our bones, but . . .' " Corky started to transmit.

"Yeah, I know. 'But names will never kill us,' " Toby's telepathy ruefully sent back.

CHAPTER NINE

Somewhere, behind Space and Time
Is wetter water, slimier slime.
—RUPERT BROOKE

THE LIGHT-FORCE, doggedly holding Toby and Corky, followed Blackbeard over land and sea. It seemed to the young people that they had invisible antennae that vibrated to the moods of the unpredictable, but in a way, predictable Light. They were experiencing a peculiar kind of maturity. It was as if they had been hurled into a mainstream which flowed in from distant brooks and rivulets of near childhood and coursed along with un- believable rapidity, sweeping them momentarily into un- explored lands of magical boundaries. There was bound to be some kind of bafflement, too—bafflement about the way in which their small plan was unwinding into such great consequences.

Teach's Light threw polychrome reflection-blurs through the ether. Corky's telepathy began sending:

"I don't know if the Devil really lights his way, but Blackbeard surely leads a rollicking life. I hope you've noticed that he *spends* most of his ill-gotten wealth ashore," her Thought-force gently reminded.

"But he doesn't spend all of it," Toby's telepathy re- torted. "We've seen him and his crew stash away lots of things."

"He certainly seems to lead a charmed life," Corky thought. "Looks as if no lawful authority is able to capture him. Woodes Rogers couldn't catch him in the Caribbean. Here he is back in the Carolina Province, still a-pirating to beat all get-out!"

The truth was that Blackbeard, under threats of retaliation if they did not do his bidding, compelled the planters in and around Bath and Eden Town to supply his wants. He levied heavy tolls on all vessels that came up the rivers or went down. He also raided the small trading ships on the North Carolina sounds—a practice that was bringing economic ruin to the small planters and traders.

The pirate avoided the Caribbean, knowing the full sweep against piracy that Woodes Rogers was exerting in that area. He used Ocracoke Inlet as his way of getting in and out of the coastal sounds. The Inlet was the main point of entry for ships sailing to the heavily populated northern part of the province; therefore, it became an ideal base for the pirate pack. It was nothing unusual for many merchant vessels to wait in its protected waters before passing out to sea. Too, the quiet waters of Pamlico Sound offered a near-perfect setting for Blackbeard to careen his ships. There were shallows there. Careening involved sailing a vessel into shallow water until it ran aground. The pirates then moved the cargo, cannon, and other gear to one side, causing the ship to lean heavily.

The tilted area exposed the hull below the waterline. The crew scraped off the barnacles and other marine encrustations which attached themselves and acted as a drag to the ships' sailing progress. They then treated the hulls of the vessels with a daubing of tallow and sulphur. Because Blackbeard's ships sailed in tropical waters as well as up and down the North American coast, it was necessary to careen the ships as often as three or four times a year.

The deep channel close to Ocracoke Inlet Blackbeard had discovered early. He realized that it was a very safe place for his ships to anchor in the event that his vessels had to make a fast getaway. The channel came to be called Teach's Hole. After each careening, the pirate made sure that all his ships lay anchored there.

The Ocracoke waters gradually became a popular sanctuary for corsairs other than Blackbeard. Because of stricter surveillance on the seas and tighter security around the ports, pirate nests had been practically cleaned out in New Providence, Philadelphia, New York City, and Newport, Rhode Island. Blackbeard and his men, in August, had landed at Philadelphia and, as they had done in the past, stridden cockily along the streets. A warrant for their arrest issued by the governor of Pennsylvania sent them scurrying to their ship and sailing back to the Carolina coast. Now, Blackbeard realized that the Carolina province was about the only place in the colonies where a pirate could find refuge. Because of geography, politics, and his devious shrewdness, Blackbeard felt that he was fortunate in having picked Ocracoke as his lair.

On Ocracoke Island, then, the pirate chose his hiding place. He and his crews made it their business to learn everything there was to know about the sandbars, the channels, and the shoals of the surrounding waters. The pilots became adept at navigating the pirate vessels through the obstructions to the safety of deep water.

Past the Inlet, around the southern tip of the island, Blackbeard built his Lookout Tower at Springer's Point. Men were set to watch for ships that could be caught as

prizes. The pirate gathered a store of armaments. He was determined to turn Ocracoke into a pirate empire as infamous as New Providence or Madagascar. Ocracoke would be a place of rendezvous for the Brotherhood.

"And while the Companies are in me territory, I'll be a king!" Blackbeard gloated, swelling with conceit as he strutted among his men, weaving his fantasies of power and glory. "Me fees will be a percentage of any vessel's prize in pay fer me giving sanctuary to it." His wicked, appraising mind laid dozens of devious plans. At no time had he exhibited greater ambition or more grandiose ideas and schemes. His ego told him that he was a master strategist. Even though he did not have the great number of crewmen he usually employed, he knew he had capable, trustworthy pirate help. So, here on Ocracoke and its nearby waters, he determined to be the greatest pirate who sailed the seas. His conceit knew no bounds and, many times, his pirate crew were hard put to tolerate the abuses he inflicted on them.

When the time for the Ocracoke Rendezvous rolled around, it promised to be a very businesslike one because of the presence of Captain Charles Vane. Vane was noted for his no-foolishness personality. Anne Bonney, the estranged wife of "Calico Jack" Rackham, was there. She was now sailing with "Gentleman" Stede Bonnet, who was also present. "Calico Jack," after his marriage breakup, had become a lieutenant under Vane's command. He was there. And, of course, Blackbeard with his Ocracoke-based legions. Blackbeard's latest bride, Prudence, was safely stashed on his sloop anchored in Teach's Hole. Except for pirates, women had no place there. Most certainly not his new bride for every swabby to cast leering looks at!

It was late September when the Rendezvous began and into October before anyone was sober enough to handle a ship and sail out to sea. The beaches at Ocracoke, particularly around Springer's Point and down close to Teach's Hole, were peopled with buccaneers and seamen in baggy, knee-length trousers, in brash silk shirts, and in cowls of silk or cotton, which they knotted about their necks or double-twisted to support a brace of pistols, whose knotted butts shone against jeweled earrings worth a king's ransom. Cutlasses were bright with oil, their sharply honed blades swinging from belted, strutting hips. Chests, arms, and faces showed conglomerations of the puckered scars of healed or healing wounds. Pirate eyes—small, large, piercing, and sun-bleached—scanned everything with leering cunning and smug mockery. The scene was like a painted canvas of landed sea wolves.

On an evening in October, the pirate conclave began. Blackbeard looked over the company that sat at the table in a room of the first story of his Lookout Tower. His diabolical, broken countenance, his sneering smiles, which showed his gold-ridged teeth, seemed at great variance with the dapper appearance of "Gentleman" Stede Bonnet, who was dressed in a waistcoat and breeches of red damask. There was a red feather in Bonnet's tricorne. Around his neck he wore a gold chain with a large diamond cross. He sported a large ruby in his right ear. Blackbeard openly sneered at Bonnet's dandyism, mentally cataloguing him for a spineless, easily-dominated swab.

Charles Vane, the cold-blooded, stony-cruel pirate of the Caribbean, was speaking, in between chewing down on a piece of roasted pig he held in both hands. Blackbeard watched Vane with gimlet eyes. He had heard that Vane might have some new ideas to propound at the Rendezvous. At the moment, however, Blackbeard's thoughts and face became sour at what he thought was Vane's arrogance and apparent bent towards dominating the meeting. This was Blackbeard's ground, and he would tolerate nobody's taking over, even a little! However, he held his peace and listened.

"This is a good rendezvous place," Vane was saying. "We should meet here at least twice a year. Assemblages like this bring the Brotherhood closer together. Times now ain't as they were before Woodes Rogers became governor. The Caribbean is already a trap for pirates."

"Hear! Hear!" The pirates lifted their flagons of rum in a nodding salute of agreement.

Blackbeard sat immobile. He did not lift his cup. His glassy, black eyes had focused on Anne Bonney who, at that moment, was opening a velvet reticule she carried on her belt.

"What's that wench up to?" he thought, frowning. He was well aware that the woman pirate had attached herself to Stede Bonnet after publicly disclaiming Jack Rackham as her husband. He knew she was ambitious and was deviously trying to get a ship for herself. Blackbeard violently disapproved of women being in the Brotherhood. At Bonnet's insistence, Anne Bonney had been included. Blackbeard had been outvoted. Ardent hate for Bonnet oozed from Blackbeard, lifting the hairs on his arms with its intensity.

Anne Bonney took out a paper, laid it down, and clapped her hands to get attention.

"What is it, Madam Rackham?" Vane asked with chilling intensity, showing his dislike for the interruption.

"Ever since I heard that you were planning to talk about pirate law at this rendezvous, I have been thinking," she replied. "And I have come to a conclusion."

Blackbeard sat up straighter. His face became a thundercloud. Was Vane brash enough to try to set up rules for *him*—for *Blackbeard—in his own diggings?* "Methinks I don't like the smell of that," he said, belching into his cup. And that strumpet Bonney—she was talking like she was the Queen of Sheba! "But I'll hold me tongue and hear the wench out," he mumbled, letting out another great burp, which sent the saliva and rum down the front of his coat. Using his sleeve, he sloughed off the worst and started picking bones from the greasy fish he held in his hands.

Anne Bonney threw a look of revulsion at Blackbeard. Her penetrating stare plainly showed that she thought him a low scoundrel with his mumbling and slobbering; that he sickened her by his filthy appearance and obnoxious habits.

Blackbeard must have felt her gaze. He looked up. But she had transferred her eyes to Stede Bonnet, who was meticulously wiping his mouth and fingers with a large square of purple linen which he had taken from his pocket.

Charles Vane had witnessed the little episode. He laid down his piece of roast pig and addressed Anne Bonney:

"And what, indeed, Madam Rackham, is the conclusion that you have reached?" he asked with curling sarcasm.

"My father was a solicitor in both Ireland and this country. I know something about legal procedure. I have made up an insurance list," she replied, looking up demurely at Vane.

"Oh?" Vane said, his interest now taking precedence over his sarcasm. Blackbeard sat glowering. He did not like what this smacked of. The wench was acting like she owned creation!

Anne Bonney picked up the piece of paper she had laid down. Without waiting for Vane's permission, she began to talk. "I believe what I have put on this list is fair to both captain and crew—it is a list of benefits for injuries received when pirate crews are under fire."

"Read your list, Madam," Vane commanded.

Blackbeard pricked up his ears. He had his own rules about such things, and he was certain that he was not going to change them. He was liking this conclave less and less.

"If a man loses a right arm in battle," Anne Bonney began to read, "he is entitled to 600 pieces of eight; if he loses a left arm, 500 pieces of eight; if he loses a right leg, 500 pieces; a left leg, 400 pieces; and the loss of any finger, 100 pieces of eight." She looked the captains squarely in the eye, folded the paper, and put it back into her reticule. She sat down and waited quietly.

"Blimey, but she's a brassy hussy," Blackbeard mumbled. He cast his black look in Vane's direction, wondering how he would take this piece of foolishness from "Calico Jack's" ex-wife.

A hush fell over the company. Vane stared intently at the woman. After a time, he picked up his rum cup and swilled down his grog. Then he addressed her:

"You've got a man's way of putting things—clean and straight with no malarkey, Madam Rackham. The list sounds sensible. We'll think on it. Now, for the edification of you greenhorn swabbies who are about to set out pirating, I, too, have a paper to read. It's called Pirate Law, and every man-jack of you will do well to memorize these laws and not forget them in the future."

With that advice, Vane began to read the age-old rules which had been set down in the beginnings of piracy. On and on, he droned out the rules. Many of the old, seasoned buccaneers took the opportunity to get up and stretch their legs. Not Blackbeard. He sat and swilled cup after cup of rum, determined to hear Vane out. Anne Bonney also kept her place at the table.

"Every Company of the Brotherhood shall swear to these laws on the Bible," Vane said, getting near the end of his list. "If there is no Bible, then the swearing will be done on a hatchet and will be just as binding." He paused as the returning, older captains again took their places at the table. "And one more thing," Vane added. "If a pirate meets a prudent woman and bothers her in any way without her consent, he shall suffer punishment by death." Vane folded his rules and put them into his pocket.

The whole company looked toward Blackbeard. They all knew his reputation for marrying. Tales had trickled out about how he treated his wives. They knew Prudence, his latest bride, was aboard ship. Nobody uttered a word. Blackbeard studiously picked bones from his sea mullet, his brain churning like a gristmill.

Anne Bonney rose. "Thank you, Captain Vane," she said, sweeping a curtsy. "Thank you for allowing me to hear the rules." She imperiously left the company, ignoring Blackbeard, the host, and made her way toward her own camp half a mile down the beach.

"What about the New England pirates?" "Calico Jack" inquired. "They have been straying out of their territories more and more lately since the cleanouts in the northern colonies."

"If there is to be booty for all, Worley, Fly, Harriot, and Moody have to stay within their bounds and take their pickings where they can find them in the northern waters," Vane said, frowning.

"Blasted buckoes! They ought to be here at this rendezvous," Blackbeard swore. "I'll not have them encroaching on me!"

Vane frowned, not liking Blackbeard's attitude. All the pirates on the North American coast had something like unofficial territories. Stede Bonnet used the waters of the southern province of Carolina, around the Cape Fear and Charles Town. Blackbeard ruled the waters of the northern province, with the Virginia capes as his northern boundary and his southern boundary the Cape Fear Shoals. If he felt inclined to pirate in Bonnet's territory, who was there to stop him! He asked no permission for anything from any man! Especially "Gentleman" Stede!

Vane saw that Blackbeard was growing quite drunk and surly. But he was hardheaded enough to realize that the Brotherhood needed what Blackbeard had to offer. Swallowing down his distaste for Blackbeard, Vane spoke:

"Captain Teach has a long list of captures," he said. "Not long ago, a London ship out of Charles Town netted him six thousand pounds. Then he grabbed Samuel Wragg and made Charles Town pay tribute to get him back. That was smart and lucrative business."

Blackbeard pricked up his ears and grinned evilly. This was more like it. It was about time Vane recognized him.

"And," Vane continued, "Captain Teach has made a friend for pirates. I refer to Governor Eden."

"And blast me eyes, iffen I don't go and come at will to the governor's summer residence at Bath Town and his palace on the Chowan," Blackbeard braggingly bawled, sloshing out his rum.

"The governor has even given Captain Teach His

Majesty's clemency without taking away his booty," Vane went on.

"Haw! Haw!" the Company shouted in glee at the thought of Blackbeard's duplicity.

"That ain't all, me hearties," Blackbeard went on, gloatingly. "That old goat, Tobias Knight, lets me have storage space fer me cargoes while he looks t'other way. Shrive his white-livered, hypocritical soul." Again, the Company bellowed, Blackbeard louder than anybody.

"Remember that," Vane said, very businesslike. "Tobias Knight is Governor Eden's secretary. He's Collector of the Port and also sits as an Admiralty judge. So, if and when we ever need one, we have a friend at court."

"What news of the Caribbean, Captain Vane?" Stede Bonnet spoke up.

"Bad tidings, indeed," Vane answered. "Woodes Rogers, the governor of New Providence, has a fleet operating against us which has about obliterated piracy in those waters. It's slim pickings, indeed. Even the smugglers are protected against us."

"What about the rumors that things are brewing ill for pirates on the North American coast?" Bonnet inquired. "I hear you had bad news out of Williamsburg, Captain Teach."

With a baleful look at the despised Bonnet, Blackbeard replied surlily:

"I sent some of me crew dressed as yeomen into Williamsburg. I, too, heered rumors."

"What did your men learn?" "Calico Jack" asked.

With a raging oath, Blackbeard smote the table, making flagons and dishes jump. "Seems that Governor Spottswood, damn his eyes, is sick of piracy. Me men heered in the taverns that the governor has guard ships and gunboats on the James and York rivers, ready to sail in an hour against any pirate in Virginia waters."

"God's breath!" Bonnet exclaimed. "Governor Johnson of the southern province has been gathering a fleet too. Can't you see their intention? He and Spottswood will have their ships meet and, in between, blast out all pirate rendezvous and hunting along the Banks and waters between Charles Town and the Virginia Capes. I say the better part of wisdom is for us *all* to sail south, to Honduras."

"What say you, Captain Teach?" Vane asked.

"Run? Turn our tails and run at the old wives' tales heered in taverns? No, blast me eyeballs, I will not run. I'll fight to the last man. But no running." His eyes became granite, holding no reflecting light or depth.

"But the Virginia governor has well-equipped ships. They are well-manned and well-gunned," Bonnet argued.

"Bah, so was your *Revenge*—well-manned and well-gunned," Blackbeard sneered. "But I took her away from ye easy enough and ye inter the bargain, didn't I? I heered ye made big boasts in Nassau—boasts how ye'd raze the towns along the Carolina coast. How ye was going to go into every river and creek and sound, despoil the plantations, and collect tribute. Seems like ye spun some old wives' tales of yer own. What's the matter, 'Gentleman' Stede? Are ye squeamish at the sight of blood?" Blackbeard roared with jeering laughter.

"Damn your eyes, Edward Teach, for such a braggart." Bonnet's temper flared out of control. He knew he was not the equal of Blackbeard in cunning, cupidity, or stark brutality, but suddenly his sword flashed in the lantern light, pricking Blackbeard's wrist before he could step backwards.

"Ye've nicked me pistol wrist," Blackbeard bellowed, going for his dirk. "I'll slit yer proud nose fer this, ye dandy fop."

"Gentlemen, keep your tongues between your teeth and hold your tempers. This is no time for disagreement within the Brotherhood," Vane snapped, stepping between them.

Bonnet bolted through the doorway, out to the beach, where he thrust his sword deep into the sand to clean the point of Blackbeard's blood. Then he angrily stalked off over the dunes, his motley crew following him to the small boats which would carry them to Bonnet's ship, the *Royal James*.

"More than ever now you have made Bonnet your enemy," Vane told Blackbeard. The Caribbean captain did not relish the incident. An important rendezvous such as this was for the purpose of gathering and giving out information for the benefit of the Brotherhood, not for settling personal animosities.

"Pah! I have a thousand enemies," Blackbeard snarled.

"I'd stay away from Charles Town and the Cape Fear. Remember, that's Bonnet's territory," Vane warned.

"Roast Bonnet's black heart!" Blackbeard roared. "I takes orders from no man alive," he hissed through slobbering lips, spitting out anger on Vane like agates on a hard floor.

Vane was hard put to hold his own temper under control. However, at this moment, he was shrewd enough to know that he must not threaten Blackbeard in his own bailiwick. As far as he could see, the Rendezvous was over. The territories were redefined, the laws laid down. He knew that he must not trust himself to stay in Blackbeard's company any longer. He turned on his heel and walked out of the Lookout Tower, his men following him. The small boats put out, taking the Caribbean captain to his ship, which lay at anchor in Teach's Hole.

"Blast and be-damn," Blackbeard bawled drunkenly. "Fall to, me hearties." The pirate's men came running from all directions. The moonlight reflected their gaudy shirts and breeches with broad sashes. "Snap to it, ye lubbers," Blackbeard screeched, "afore I takes a notion to run ye through a gauntlet of them marsh rushes on yer naked behinds! More rum, Hush Stiles. I want to wash the taste of this blasted Rendezvous out of me gullet."

Stiles came running with a leathern flask. Blackbeard held it up and imbibed a long draught. Then he used the rum to douse his nicked wrist, from which the blood still dripped.

A young seaman standing by watched Blackbeard in terrified awe.

"Billy Weems," Blackbeard bawled at the young ruffian, "ye're a stout lad with keen eyes. Put out a small boat and row me to the ship. Me new Madam awaits me." His wicked laughter echoed and re-echoed drunkenly over the bleached sands of Ocracoke.

Teach's Light, hanging high above the Lookout Tower, slowly began to sway and bob through the autumn night. Away up in space, it came to rest over Blackbeard's sloop, which was riding high on the waters of Teach's Hole.

CHAPTER TEN

Time has laid its hand.
—LONGFELLOW

MONTHS went by. Blackbeard continued to use Ocracoke as his pirate hangout. He constantly plagued the shipping on the inland waters of the coastal sounds. He kept the people in Eden Town and Bath in a perpetual state of anxiety, not knowing what kind of behavior he might exhibit or what tricks his devious mind would concoct.

One day in early November, 1718, Teach's Light suddenly streaked from over Springer's Point and settled over Pamlico Sound near Teach's Hole. Toby and Corky, constrained by the Force, saw a particularly bloody battle take place between Blackbeard's sloop and a brig out of Wilmington. The pirates cut down the hapless crew and tossed their bodies overboard. They took the cargo of white sugar and hemp. Then Blackbeard set the vessel on fire. As was the usual practice after taking a prize, the company began celebrating their victory with a drunken brawl.

"This is a nightmare," Toby's Thought-force angrily transmitted. There seemed to have made up within him some kind of new, controlled violence—a passion to strike out at the way Blackbeard played with human life. "I'd like to get my hands in that matted hair and drag that pirate through a field of cockleburs," he transmitted furiously.

"Whoa, there," Corky admonished. "Don't you know that hatred is a live, insidious thing that curls around you, creeps into you, and lies heavily against your heart? The receiver of hate generally has reasons to 'do in' the hater, too." However, her own perceptions churned with a quiet boil. "I imagine Edward Teach intends to take over Hades if anything happens to Satan. He seems to exist in a cycle that swings between terror and civility, sanity and insanity."

"The folks in the colony have just got to do something," Toby's senses wailed. "How much more pirate treachery can they take?"

News of the capture and burning of the Wilmington brig spread over the coastal towns like wildfire. The people of the province were up in arms. They had had enough of Blackbeard and his cutthroats! But what to do? The merchants and shipowners knew that it was useless to apply to Governor Eden. Governor Johnson of the southern province had his hands full with Indian troubles and with his own pirates. There was no help in that quarter. So, the North Carolinians took their plea to Governor Spottswood of Virginia.

The Virginia governor referred the matter to captains George Gordon of HMS *Pearl* and Ellis Brand of HMS

Lyme, two British frigates then lying in the James River for the protection of Virginia's trade.

Gordon and Brand were aware of Blackbeard's depredations in Carolina. However, they knew that their frigates were too large to get at the pirate vessels that frequented the shallow sounds. It was determined, finally, that two small sloops would be sent from Virginia to be manned and armed from the frigates. Robert Maynard, first lieutenant of His Majesty's Ship *Pearl*, would command.

Again, the pirate grapevine buzzed. Blackbeard received a letter from Tobias Knight, telling him of the rumors coming down from Virginia. He even intimated that he was dispatching to Ocracoke four of Blackbeard's pirates that were in Bath. He warned Blackbeard to be on guard.

The pirate had received many similar reports in the past from ships that came into Ocracoke—reports which had been proved false; therefore, he gave these new reports no credence at all, swearing that he would not be intimidated by a "bloody lot of palaverings and old wives' tales." He might have done well had he listened and heeded. But he did not. He wore his arrogance like an armor and, as usual, did as he jolly well pleased.

On November 21, 1718, two sloops, the *Ranger*, with a picked crew of twenty-two men under the captaincy of a Mr. Hyde, and the larger of the sloops, with a crew of thirty-two, under the personal command of Lieutenant Maynard, reached Ocracoke Inlet.

Blackbeard saw the sloops.

It was then, for the first time, that credence in the reports he had heard began to sink in. However, he still showed very little concern. He certainly showed no fear.

It was evening when Maynard and Hyde arrived at the Inlet. They saw that the place was full of shoals, that the channel was too intricate to navigate at night, and that it would be foolhardy to try to engage Teach until the daylight hours. They anchored.

Night fell deep and gentle over the placid waters and bleached sands of Ocracoke. The glow of lanterns from the few anchored ships in the sound bobbed up and down through the darkness like lazy June bugs.

But one vessel anchored in Teach's Hole was a beehive of activity—Blackbeard's sloop.

The pirate swilled rum and worked his men like demons, putting his ship in a posture of defense. As they had done in their battle with the *Scarborough* and in many other battles, gun crews began to pack hammocks, bedding, and seabags into nets.

"Avast, mateys," Blackbeard commanded in a tempered-down voice. It was a calm night, and the pirate knew that speech carried over water. This time he did not aim to advertise what he was doing. He cautioned quiet among his men. "When I used the long glass afore nightfall, I seed no big guns mounted on them sloops out there. I want ye to make grenadoes first, afore ye bother stowing things. We'll stow later. More rum, Hush Stiles! And Phil Morton, bring up powder and cartridges and scrap iron. Git a hundred of them case bottles from the hold. Stuff them full of black powder, scrap iron, slugs, small shot, and pieces of lead. Fall to, Richard Greensail, and fetch up them quick matches from the galley."

Hush Stiles returned with the rum. Blackbeard tilted the bottle and guzzled it like a man dying of thirst.

Stiles watched him. A frown of worry played across his grizzled face. "Cap'n," he spoke hesitatingly. Even though he had known Teach for many years, he still was never sure of Blackbeard's reactions. "Cap'n," he began again.

"Spit it out, Stiles, and stop yer gibbering," Blackbeard told him.

"Cap'n, we ain't got but twenty-five men. Hadn't we orter try to make a run fer it?" he asked fearfully.

"Be-damn'd to ye, Hush Stiles," Blackbeard spat out. "Ye ain't never seen me run yet, have ye? Besides, I've told everybody around these diggings we got forty men or more. Every vessel I've spoke with fer two weeks or longer thinks our strength is great. No, by damn, we don't run!" With that, the pirate upended the rum bottle and swigged down the rest of the grog. "Fetch me another!" Blackbeard commanded. "And don't ye worry none, old matey."

"Aye, aye, Cap'n," Stiles replied, making his way toward the galley. But the worry still remained imbedded on his countenance.

Finally, the pirates finished all the tasks that Blackbeard had set them to do. The pirate ship was in readiness and armed to the teeth. Blackbeard commanded his men to quarters.

"Rest and quiet, me hearties," he admonished them. "The night wanes and the morrow approaches, with what fortunes no man can foretell. We be ready and able fer it. And be-damn'd to any rogue who says me various." With those words, he took three large flagons of rum and strode into his own quarters. It was nothing short of amazing that he had any coordination at all, considering the amount of raw spirits he had already drunk. But he seemed entirely unaffected by his draughts. "Blast me eyes," he swore. "Me bloody log. I ain't writ it fer the day." He took the log off a chest and sat down and began to write:

Such a day—Company somewhat sober—but a damn'd Confusion among us because of two strange vessels in Inlet—great talk of British sloops come to nab Blackbeard in his lair: kept Company hot making grenadoes and packing guns—aim to make somebody's skin hot, damn'd hot, on the morrow iffen they tangle with Blackbeard: Eight Bells. All's well.

He put the log back on the chest, took his three flagons of rum, and went to the deck of the sloop.

During the midnight hours, Blackbeard paced the deck of his vessel and drank rum. As the night waned, he began to swear great maudlin oaths, his voice raspy and getting louder and louder.

"Oh, crow cock!" he bawled dozens of times, cursing the dawn that seemed to be coming at a snail's pace. He shook his fists in the direction of the anchored British vessels, calling down imprecations on the brilliant star which hung over them.

When the first rays of morning appeared over Ocracoke, the British sloops made their move. Their rigging gleamed silver against a sky so blue that it looked as if it had been swept by an angel's broom. Slowly and doggedly the vessels made their way toward Blackbeard's ship.

Overhead, near the stratosphere, Teach's Light followed the British sloops. Its brilliance, as was usual, had dimmed. Corky and Toby, held inexorably, began experiencing a hyperesthesia that was tinged with wild, fearful exhilaration.

Using great prudence, Lieutenant Maynard sent out a small boat from his sloop to sound the shoals. When it came within gunshot range, Blackbeard fired upon it.

"Hoist the flag! His Majesty's colors!" Maynard commanded. Both his sloops immediately complied. Maynard's vessel stood directly toward Blackbeard's ship.

"Cut the blasted cable, Gibbens," Blackbeard commanded the boatswain. "We'll make a bloody, running fight of it. Blast 'em with constant fire from the big guns,

Philip Morton," he squalled to the gunner. "Give 'em a taste of Blackbeard's Hell!"

The lieutenant had no big guns, as Blackbeard had correctly surmised the night before. But Maynard and most of his crew kept up a constant barrage with small arms at the pirate ship, while some of the lieutenant's men labored with the oars. The waters were strange and tricky to them. They had to be careful.

Back and forth, through the shoals, the ships swung. Blackbeard ran aground. The pirate swore great oaths and belabored his crew, calling down maledictions for his plight.

Maynard's vessel drew more water than the pirate sloop; therefore, he could not come any nearer. He anchored within half a gunshot range.

"Throw out the ballast," Maynard ordered. "Stave the water!" When his vessel was lightened, the lieutenant weighed anchor and headed for Blackbeard.

The pirate ran to the side of his sloop, shrieking blistering oaths and blasphemy:

"Damn ye fer villains! Who are ye? From whence come ye?"

"You can see by our colors that we're not pirates," Maynard retorted.

"Send that small boat on board, blast ye, so I can see *who* ye are. Send her alongside," Blackbeard called, trying out his famous "con" on the lieutenant. He knew his pirates would make mincemeat of the oarsmen if they came close enough to his ship.

But Maynard would have none of Blackbeard's chicanery. "I cannot spare my boat. But as soon as I think feasible, I'll come aboard you with my sloop," Maynard promised, in a threatening tone.

Blackbeard grabbed a bottle of rum held out to him by one of the crewmen. He upended the bottle and swilled it down, except for the last mouthful, which he arrogantly spat over the water in Maynard's direction.

"Damnation seize me soul," he roared, "if I give quarter or take it from the likes of ye!"

"I expect no quarter," Maynard retorted. "Neither will you get any from me."

Suddenly a great shout went up from the pirate ship. Blackbeard's sloop had floated off the shoal.

Maynard's vessels rowed toward the sloop. His crewmen were exposed from the waist up.

"Blast the bloody rogues with a broadside," Blackbeard squalled. He was in high glee. His ship was clear. The fight was shaping up to his liking. The bloodlust burned hot within him.

The pirate's broadside, charged with all manner of small shot, struck both the British sloops. On Maynard's vessel, twenty men fell wounded or dead. On the *Ranger*, Hyde and eight of his crew were killed. The terrible situation could not have been avoided. There was no wind for the sails; so, the lieutenant's men found it necessary to keep to their oars else Blackbeard would get away. That was a possibility Lieutenant Maynard was determined to prevent. But he knew that Blackbeard had dealt him a telling blow.

Blackbeard's helmsmen steered the pirate parallel to the shore. The *Ranger*, disabled for the present, fell astern. Maynard, seeing that his own ship had way, knew he would soon come alongside Blackbeard. Hastily spot-checking his able crewmen, the lieutenant ordered them to the hold of the ship. He feared another broadside. If that occurred, it would certainly destroy him and lose him the prospect of catching the pirate. All the live crewmen, with the exception of the helmsman and Maynard, hastened to the hold of the sloop.

"Load your pistols. See to your swords," Maynard directed them. "Be ready for close infighting. Place two ladders in the hatchway," he went on, "and come up at my command." To the helmsman, he directed: "Lie down flat, out of sight, with your sword and pistol at the ready."

Maynard's sloop and Blackbeard's vessel bumped together.

"The grenadoes! Hurl the grenadoes!" Blackbeard shouted.

The pirates flung the bottle-grenades, dozens of them. The quick-lighting matches fired the black powder within the bottles as they were thrown. The grenades were deadly. They also had the added effect of throwing a crew into confusion. But here, on Maynard's ship, the project was wasted since the lieutenant's men were down in the hold.

Small patches of clearing appeared in the smoke, and Blackbeard saw there were only two men left on the deck of the British sloop—the helmsman and Maynard.

"They're all knocked on their bloody noggins," he roared with exultation. "Come on, me hearties. Let's jump aboard and slit the rogues' gizzards!"

Under cover of the grenade smoke, which had settled heavily over the bow, Blackbeard and fourteen of his men boarded the lieutenant's sloop.

"NOW!" Maynard shouted, signaling his men.

Up the ladders and out of the hatch came Maynard's men, their sabers glittering in the bright sunlight.

Instantly, Blackbeard and Maynard fired at each other.

Blackbeard was hit. Blood streamed from his wound. "Damn yer eyeballs, ye lily-livered villain," Blackbeard snarled, grabbing for his cutlass. "I'll cut out yer black heart and feed it to the ravens," he bawled, making a great lunge toward Maynard.

Maynard met the charge. But his sword broke. He threw down the broken blade and stepped back to cock his pistol.

With a swinging, deadly aim of the cutlass, Blackbeard

bore in toward the lieutenant. One of Maynard's men swung down with his sword, giving Blackbeard a terrible wound in the neck and throat. This action saved Maynard. He received only a small cut on his fingers. Blackbeard was a ghastly spectacle of streaming gore. Yet, he stubbornly fought on.

The sunlight on the blue waters of Pamlico Sound mirrored the flashing blades of cutlass, poniard, and dirk. Lieutenant Maynard had twelve men. Blackbeard had fourteen. The engagement on the slimy, blood-covered deck of the British sloop was ragingly hot. The tough skulls of the weathered seamen echoed and re-echoed the constant blows. Pistol fire crackled through the morning air. Bloodshed, butchery, carnage, and havoc were the scene. Blood ran down the scuppers of Maynard's vessel, and the waters around it became tinctured with gore.

The lieutenant knew he had met his match. In close fighting he found Blackbeard a man to be reckoned with. Again, Maynard fired his pistol, and the pirate received the bullet in his body. Yet, Blackbeard stood his ground. Twenty times he was slashed by cutlass, poniard, or dirk by Maynard and his men. Five times his body received shots. When once again he stepped back to cock his pistol, Blackbeard fell—stone dead—to the deck of Maynard's ship.

On the slippery, bloody deck, Maynard moved in closer and looked down at the grisly figure of Edward Teach lying before him.

"So this was Blackbeard," he thought grimly. "Brother of the Devil—more myth than man. But a worthy adversary in a fight." He turned to the helmsman and said: "Give me your sword."

The helmsman handed it over.

With a quick chop, like the well-oiled motion of a

guillotine, Maynard slashed off Blackbeard's head. He carried the ghastly object to the bowsprit of his vessel, where he affixed it for all to see.

"Throw the body overboard," the lieutenant commanded.

No sooner said than two crewmen tossed the horror over the side of the sloop.

The headless body of Blackbeard splashed down into the bloody waters of Teach's Hole.

Abruptly, Toby's and Corky's telepathic senses registered a violent sundering from the Light-force. Their junction completely disintegrated, sending them whirling around in the coldness of nothing. It was as if they were impetuously dashed beyond the bounds of any zone of perception across an immensity too great for thought to traverse. But vaguely, through a great, numbing, falling sense of terror, their perceptions seemed to record an image of some macabre, headless Thing, madly swimming around a ship that lay in a sea of blood-red water. A kind of silent chant—"Seven times around! Seven times around!"—dinned through their synapses.

High up in the firmament, above the crimsoned waters of Ocracoke, a faint ball of light appeared. For a split-second it hovered over Teach's Hole. Then, like a spent-out flare, it vanished.

CHAPTER ELEVEN

*The flowers appear on the earth; the Time of the singing
of birds is come; and the voice of the dove is heard in our
land.*
—SONG OF SOLOMON 2:12

*Time engenders forgetfulness; but it does so by setting us
bodily free from our surroundings and giving us back our
primitive, unattached state.*
—THOMAS MANN

THERE commenced within Corky's and Toby's subconscious a feeling of free fall like that of sky jumpers
just before the opening of their parachutes. A complexity
of emotions, memories, hopes, and disassociated experi-
ences struggled to sort themselves out. Kaleidoscopic
patterns agitated their senses, shifting from one set of
erratic connections to a wildly deviating group of rela-
tions.

Perplexity about their surroundings settled dully on
the edge of their vague awareness. The evening glow
seemed to vanish into a totally empty distance of black-
ness so oppressive that the air felt like a heavy wall against
them. Then, visibility reappeared in the form of a red
moon, which lazily climbed and rhythmically dipped like
a bouncing ball over a page of music notes. Or was it the
sun that bleached the high, blue sky and, even now, was

turning the white cirrus clouds into scampering mares'-tails of pink and lavender?

There was color everywhere—color from camellias, whose bushes reared head-tall out of white narcissi beds. Primulas and sea pinks nodded under cattail trees which stood at attention. Rainbows hovered about them as though the angels were using giant prisms to disperse the great brilliance above them.

"It's a psychedelic stroboscope," Toby's thought processes sparked. "And my stomach's down in my toes," he thought crazily.

"It's Teach's Light," Corky undertook to transmit. "Teach's Light has turned us loose!" But communication by telepathy had vanished. She tried collecting her agitated mind, gathering scraps of energy so that she could take herself firmly in hand, but her body chemistry was at a low ebb and would not operate competently. A mixture of will and lassitude battled within. Will demanded order; languor commanded her not to move—not ever—for fear of breaking into small pieces, for fear of losing her own image in the shattered mirror of Time. She had the dizzy sensation of standing high on a cliff, looking down at two people—herself and Toby—on a solitary path. Nobody else was anywhere. Yet she and Toby walked apart, each alone near a roaring sea. They seemed tied like stones on a short chain—unable to move together, because Time was standing still.

Silly images tick-tack-toed across Toby's vision. A

white tombstone abruptly appeared before him and faded out like subliminal advertising on television. "Hah! Prudence's Pylon," he thought, with an inner giggle—a giggle that was instantaneously cut off by some power that would not tolerate such rank foolishness. The truth was that Toby's mind was in such a violent whirlpool of disorder that absolutely nothing made any sense at all. Even the air now had the effect of velvet—like cat fur rubbing his cheeks. A gentle breeze stirred the vines, making a multitude of insects chirp—insects that, he knew by all nature, should not make a chirp until July, at least. "Katydids in April," his telepathy snorted weakly. "Maybe they think it's Julember!"

There came a *sound*. Of soft music.

Corky was low-toning the melody of "The King's Navee," making up her own words. Her voice, oddly clear and firm in a light, hoarse way, slurred faintly as she sang. Even though her telepathic powers were spent, she was aware of all sorts of new wisdom which struggled within her. Faint sparks flared intermittently through all her synapses, making her feel the turmoil Toby was experiencing. She tried desperately to communicate encouragement to her friend. With something exceeding ordinary human power, she geared her mind, *willing* the ESP to return. Her effort met with failure. The telepathy would not come back.

Suddenly, it seemed that pandemonium smote the air. Jagged streaks of lightning seemed to appear. They bombarded to fragments the rainbows of color. Sounds, like ocean breakers hitting the beach in a hurricane, struck Toby's and Corky's senses like stallions charging down blind trails.

And just as abruptly, there came a quiet hush—as if Mother Nature had slipped in and swept away all discord with a duster made of gosling down.

CHAPTER TWELVE

Time cools; Time clarifies; no mood can be maintained quite unaltered through the course of Time.
—THOMAS MANN

We belong to tread a way none trod before,
But find the excellent old way through love
And through the care of children to the hour
For bidding Fate and Time and Change good-by.
—WILLIAM BUTLER YEATS

TEACH'S LIGHT hung over the clearing in Little Dismal with the arrogance of a midday sun in August.

On the edge of the clearing, Sven—or what was left of the big Norwegian—lay. One severed, mangled hand still grasped the handle of a twisted, gray box lid.

The circumstances looked very clear. The "Mad Russian's" secret box had held World War II explosives—explosives which he had jealously hoarded, hidden, and guarded for over thirty years. On this night, it was very probable that Sven's psychotic rage had driven him to bring out the explosives from their hiding place for the express purpose of annihilating once and for all the hated *Allemands* who, in the guise of Teach's Light, had appeared in the sky, riding their brilliant iron birds to threaten him all over again. On this night, he had moved against the despised Germans—Germans who had invaded his beloved country of Norway, killed his family, and sunk his ship beneath him off Cape Hatteras!

Sven's mangled body, strewn over the ground and among the weeds of the torn-up earth, was incontrovertible evidence that the secret box had exploded. Perhaps, in the dim moonlight, in trying to keep abreast of Toby and Corky, Sven had tripped and fallen, thus setting off the explosives. On seeing Teach's Light bobbing up and down over the swamp, perhaps his madness had intensified into a stroke of apoplexy which had struck him to the ground and so set off the holocaust. Mercifully, the low-lying shrubs and undergrowth, which had been torn up and uprooted, hid most of the gruesome sight of the "Mad Russian's" ghastly end on earth.

Corky, on the opposite side of the clearing, struggled to move. It was a nearly impossible task. Dirt and branches covered her. Her body felt contorted and broken into a hundred pieces, as if each piece were a roaring, pounding skull. But within her burned a great consciousness of mind that was as clear and sharp as pure crystal.

Toby, lying near her, practically buried by roots, mud, and cypress boughs, came to in a fit of sneezing which threatened to jerk his throbbing head right off his banged-up body. Mingled feelings of shock, loss, and panic coursed through him. Like a triphammer, one question pounded his brain: Had he and Corky really traveled, *in one night, three hundred years backward in Time?*

Or was all this a horrible dream—some allegory of the unconscious? His memory struggled. It was next to impossible to sort anything out.

Concussion churned their brains; so, it was some moments before Corky and Toby reached a fair state of awareness. The choking stench of gas and sulphur fumes hung about them, constricting their breathing. Both the young people seemed to be intact, with no broken bones, and no bloody wounds. Their faces were scratched and dirty; their clothing ripped. The fact that they had been on the opposite side of the clearing from the explosion had certainly saved their lives; there was no doubt of that. In short, both of the youngsters were living evidence of a rare thing—the miracle that sometimes happens once in a lifetime.

Toby pulled his hands out of the muck. They were scratched, and his nails had dug nearly through his palms. Something round, bright and shiny caught at his wavering vision. Groggily, he reached over and managed to pick up the shining object.

"Wow!" he croaked, in a haggard voice. Awe spread across his dirty face.

Corky, pushing the branches away, came up to a swaying, sitting position. She let out a strangled sort of squeal. "Man alive! Will you look!" Shock, churning insides, and a pounding head made it nearly impossible for her to get her eyes focused on the several pieces of gold money lying scattered about her. Reflections from the shimmering pieces united with the brilliance that showered down from above.

Complete wonder shone on the faces of both young people as they half-sat, half-reclined in the torn-up earth of the clearing. Suddenly, Teach's Light darted down like a mad wasp. It did a wild Devil Dance, sending down its magnificent legs of lucency to a shallow, jagged hole in the rumpled earth. In the rough concavity, Corky and Toby saw the shattered remains of what once might have been a wooden chest. About the hole, and in it, lay a few more pieces of the golden money.

A millisecond of the old telepathy seemed to flash through both of them simultaneously. They read each other's mind, and the message was transparently clear.

"What is there left to say?" Toby asked, shaking his head in wonder.

Corky looked at him and nodded solemnly—a gesture which held a thousand unspoken answers.

"Well," she said, grinning lopsidedly, "I *say*, I bet you a Coke your dad is on his way to Casey's Point to hunt for us. If he comes and finds us, what shall we tell *him*?"

"What's to tell?" Toby grinned back, answering her question with a loaded question of his own.

They shielded their eyes and looked at Teach's Light, which was now bouncing lazily away over the trees of Little Dismal.

"Do you reckon that crazy Light will be bobbing around for another three hundred years?" Toby asked.

"Well . . ." Corky started to answer, but she was interrupted by a familiar, raucous sound which tore the air—a sound like full-bellied bobcat laughter—laughter that seemed to hold a jeer and offer a promise.

Abruptly, Teach's Light dimmed. Then it quickly disappeared, leaving over the trees a smoky wreath, whose ragged edges looked for all the world like the tendrils of a long, black beard.

PIRATES KILLED IN THE ENGAGEMENT AT OCRACOKE IN NOVEMBER, 1718*

EDWARD TEACH, Commander
PHILIP MORTON, Gunner
GARRAT GIBBENS, Boatswain
OWEN ROBERTS, Carpenter
THOMAS MILLER, Quartermaster
JOHN HUSK
JOSEPH CURTICE
JOSEPH BROOKS
NATH. JACKSON

All the rest, except the two last, were wounded, and afterwards hanged in Virginia.

JOHN CARNES	JOSEPH PHILIPS
JOSEPH BROOKS	JAMES ROBBINS
JAMES BLAKE	JOHN MARTIN
JOHN GILLS	EDWARD SALTER
THOMAS GATES	STEPHEN DANIEL
JAMES WHITE	RICHARD GREENSAIL
RICHARD STILES	ISRAEL HANDS (Pardoned)
CAESAR (Negro pirate)	SAMUEL ODELL (Acquitted)

*Daniel Defoe, *A General History of the Pyrates*, edited by Manuel Schonhorn (Columbia, South Carolina: University of South Carolina Press, 1972), p. 86.

SUGGESTIONS FOR FURTHER READING

Carris, Joan Davenport. *Brethren of the Black Flag.* Danville, Va.: Coastal Plains, 1982.

Carse, Robert. *The Age of Piracy.* New York: Grosset & Dunlap, 1965.

Cordingly, David. *Under the Black Flag: The Romance and the Reality of Life Among the Pirates.* San Diego: Harcourt Brace, 1997.

Day, Jean. *Blackbeard, Terror of the Seas.* Newport, N.C.: Golden Age Press, 1997.

Defoe, Daniel. *The Life and Strange Surprising Adventures of Robinson Crusoe, of York, Mariner.* Edited by J. Donald Crowley. New York: Oxford University Press, 1998.

Fletcher, Inglis. *Lusty Wind for Carolina.* Atlanta: Cherokee Pub. Co., 1991.

Gosse, Philip. *The History of Piracy.* Glorieta, N.Mex.: Rio Grande Press, 1990.

———. *The Pirates' Who's Who.* Glorieta, N.Mex.: Rio Grande Press, 1988.

Harden, John. *The Devil's Tramping Ground.* Chapel Hill: University of North Carolina Press, 1980.

Hughes, Richard. *A High Wind in Jamaica.* London: Harvill, 1998.

Johnson, Captain Charles. *A General History of the Robberies and Murders of the Most Notorious Pirates.* Originally published in London, 1724. Edited by Arthur L. Haywood. London: Routledge and Kegan Paul, Ltd., 1955. Attributed to Daniel

Defoe and republished as *A General History of the Pyrates*. Edited by Manuel Schonhorn. Columbia, S.C.: University of South Carolina Press, 1972.

Lane, Kris E. *Pillaging the Empire: Piracy in the Americas, 1500–1750*. Armonk, N.Y.: M. E. Sharpe, 1998.

Lee, Robert Earl. *Blackbeard the Pirate: A Reappraisal of His Life and Times*. Winston-Salem, N.C.: John F. Blair, 1990.

Masefield, John. *On the Spanish Main*. London: Conway Maritime Press, Ltd., 1972.

Miers, Earl Schenk. *Pirate Chase*. Williamsburg, Va.: Colonial Williamsburg, distributed by Holt, Rinehart & Winston, New York, 1965.

Price, Jeramie. *Blackbeard's Bride*. New York: Pocket Books, 1960.

Pringle, Patrick. *Jolly Roger: The Story of the Great Age of Piracy*. New York: W. W. Norton & Co., 1953.

Rankin, Hugh F. *The Golden Age of Piracy*. New York: Holt, Rinehart & Winston, 1969.

———. *The Pirates of Colonial North Carolina*. Raleigh: N.C. State Dept. of Archives and History, 1994.

Rediker, Marcus Buford. *Between the Devil and the Deep Blue Sea: Merchant Seamen, Pirates, and the Anglo-American Maritime World, 1700–1750*. New York: Cambridge University Press, 1993.

Roberts, Nancy. *Blackbeard and Other Pirates of the Atlantic Coast*. Winston-Salem, N.C.: John F. Blair, 1993.

Whedbee, Charles Harry. *Blackbeard's Cup and Stories of the Outer Banks*. Winston-Salem, N.C.: John F. Blair, 1989.

Whipple, A. B. C. *Pirate: Rascals of the Spanish Main*. New York: Doubleday, 1961.

———. *Famous Pirates of the New World*. New York: Random House, 1958.

ACKNOWLEDGMENTS

THE AUTHOR wishes to express her grateful acknowledgment and appreciation to the Honorable Nick Galifianakis, past member of the United States House of Representatives, and his staff, for the information they sent her from the Library of Congress; to Dr. John L. Lochhead, Librarian of the Mariners Museum at Newport News, Virginia, for the photocopies of pages from the *Dictionary of National Biography* and *Jolly Roger, The Story of the Great Age of Piracy*; to David Stick, the scholarly Dare County historian, for all the documented history he has put down in his book, *The Outer Banks of North Carolina*; to writers Jeramie Price, Shirley Hughson, Robert Carse, James Burney, Phillip Gosse, A. B. C. Whipple, and Earl Schenck Miers for their great pirate stories; to Hugh Rankin for his learned book, *Pirates in Colonial North Carolina*; to the British Museum Library, the Imperial War Museum Library, and the National Maritime Museum in London, England; to Mrs. Ivadeen Westcott, Assistant Librarian in the Dare County Library in Manteo; to Bob, her longsuffering, retired navy man husband, who always helps with the seafaring lingo; to her daughter Marcia, who supplied the germ of the idea that made the book; to all her science teachers both in public school and in the universities; and certainly to all her junior-high-school science students, who made up imaginative stories about flying saucers and little green men with beeping antennas.